Benjamin Franklin Taylor

Dulce Domum

The Burden of the Song

Benjamin Franklin Taylor

Dulce Domum
The Burden of the Song

ISBN/EAN: 9783743388543

Manufactured in Europe, USA, Canada, Australia, Japa

Cover: Foto ©Andreas Hilbeck / pixelio.de

Manufactured and distributed by brebook publishing software (www.brebook.com)

Benjamin Franklin Taylor

Dulce Domum

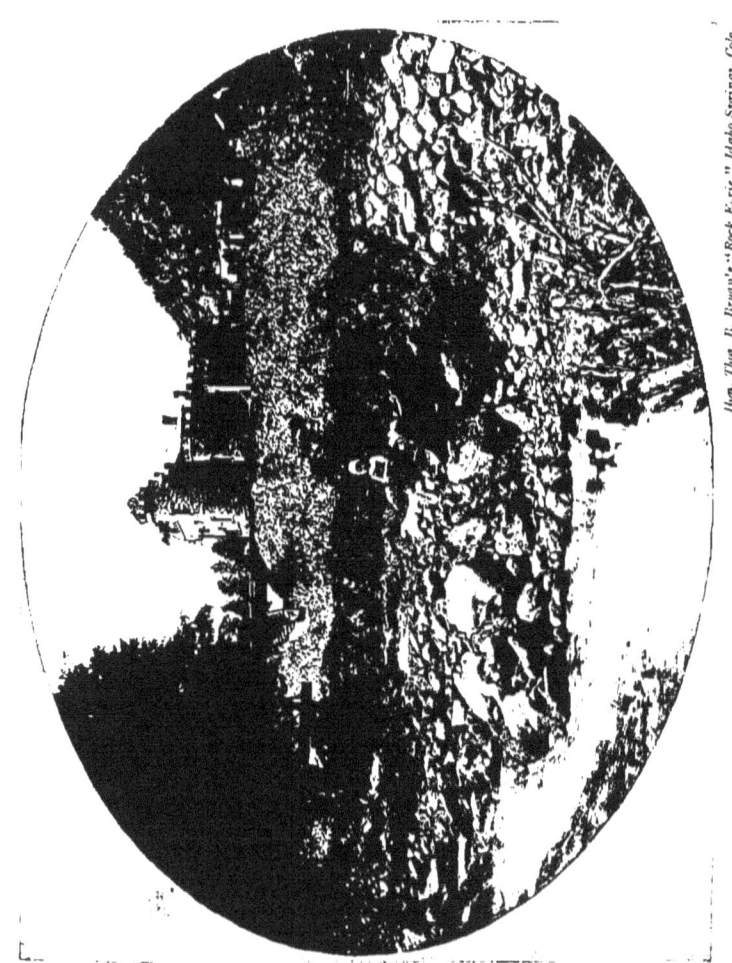

Hon. Thos. B. Bryan's "Rock Eyrie," Idaho Springs, Colo.

'MID NATURE'S HIGH RELIEF, ROCK EYRIE, HAIL!

DULCE DOMUM

THE BURDEN OF THE SONG.

By BENJ. F. TAYLOR, LL.D.,

AUTHOR OF "SONGS OF YESTERDAY," "OLD TIME PICTURES," ETC.

CHICAGO:
S. C. GRIGGS AND COMPANY.
1884.

PRESS OF
KNIGHT & LEONARD
CHICAGO

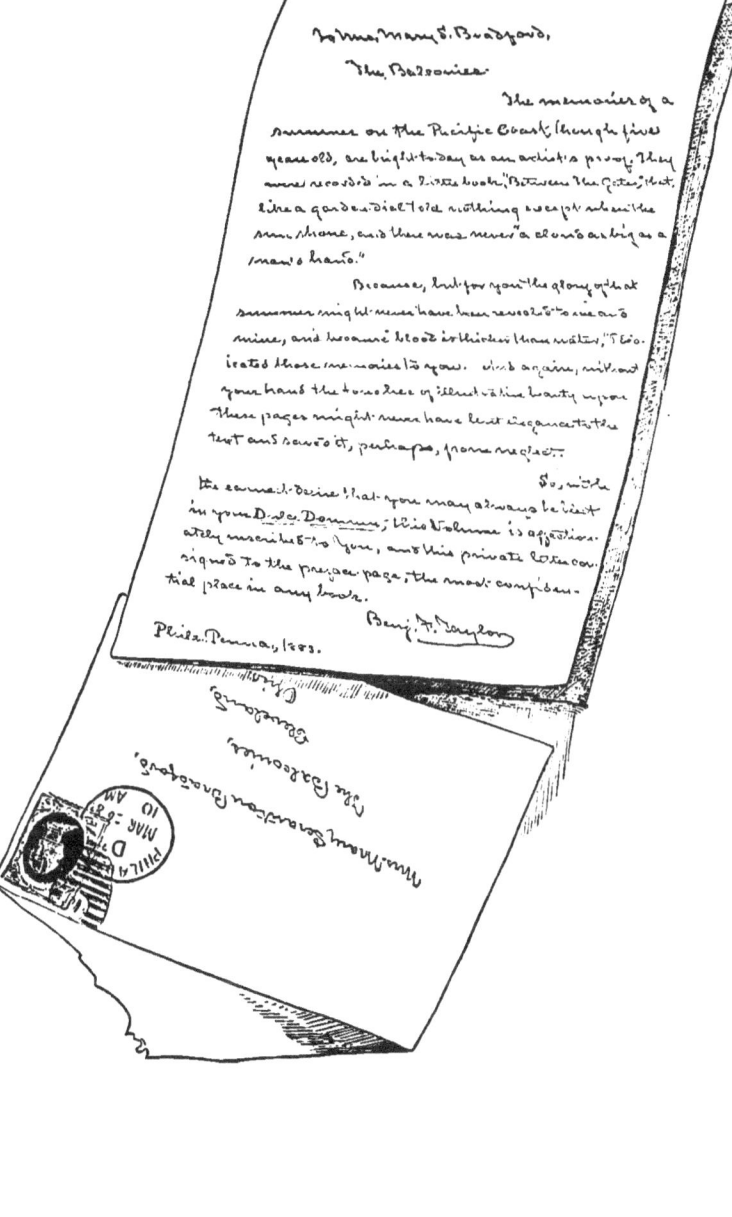

To Mrs. Mary S. Bradford,

The Balconies—

The memories of a summer on the Pacific Coast, though five years old, are bright to-day as an artist's proof. They were recorded in a little book, "Between The Gates," that, like a garden dial, told nothing except when the sun shone, and there was never a cloud as big as a man's hand."

Because, but for you the glory of that summer might never have been revealed to me and mine, and because blood is thicker than water, I dedicated those memories to you. And again, without your hand the touches of illustrative beauty upon these pages might never have lent elegance to the text and saved it, perhaps, from neglect.

So, with the earnest desire that you may always be best in your Dolce Domum, this Volume is affectionately inscribed to you, and this private letter consigned to the proper page, the most confidential place in any book.

Benj. F. Taylor

Phila. Penna., 1883.

Mrs. Mary Bradford Bradford,
The Balconies,
Cleveland,
Ohio.

PHILA. D. MAR 7 83 10 AM

CONTENTS.

THE SUN THAT NEVER SETS, - - - - - - - 1

NEW YORK "NORTH WOODS," - - - - - 9

THE CAPTAIN'S DRUM, - - - - - - 21

HEARTS AND HEARTHS, - - - - - - 29

A LAMENT FOR ADAM, - - - - - - - 35

"DON'T GIVE UP THE SHIP," - - - - 39

LINCOLN AND HIS PSALM, - - - - - - 45

THE TWO ARMIES, - - - - - - - 49

ROSE, LILY AND MAY FLOWER, - - - - - 51

MASSACHUSETTS SENDS GREETING, - - - - 55

"GOD KNOWS," - - - - - - - - 61

THISTLE SERMON, - - - - - - - 65

A BIRTH-DAY, - - - - - - - - 67

ROCK EYRIE, - - - - - - - 72

THE FLYING HERALDS, - - - - - - - 73

AUGUST LILIES, -   -   -   -   -   -   -   -   83

CENTENNIAL BELLS, -   -   -   -   -   -   -   87

TWO RIVERS AND TWO SHIPS,   -   -   -   -   -   95

OLD-FASHIONED SPRING,   -   -   -   -   -   -   101

ONE STEP MORE,   -   -   -   -   -   -   -   107

THE BEAUTY OF DEATH,   -   -   -   -   -   -   113

THE CALIFORNIA YEAR, -   -   -   -   -   -   -   119

A VISION OF HANDS,   -   -   -   -   -   -   125

"AND FORBID THEM NOT,"   -   -   -   -   -   -   133

PRAIRIE LAND,   -   -   -   -   -   -   -   135

THE DESERTED HOMESTEAD,   -   -   -   -   -   -   139

THE GARDEN THERMOMETER,   -   -   -   -   -   149

THE MINGLING OF THE NATIONS,   -   -   -   -   -   151

WELCOME HOME,   -   -   -   -   -   -   -   155

"Rock Eyrie, hail!" - - - - - - *Frontispiece*

"Maine and Alaska hand in hand,
The self-same hour behold in one
A rising and a setting sun!" - - - - - 5

Flowers, - - - - - - - - 8

A Big "Major" of Bears, - - - - - 12

A Pioneer, - - - - - - - - 13

"Ah, as fine and as clear as a sunlit vignette
Is the office whence came The Black River Gazette," - 14

A "Spot" in the Wilderness, - - - - 17

Some Wilderness Weather, - - - - 19

"'Twas double-drag and Holy Word,
Thus saith the drum and thus the Lord," - - - 27

"For up the sweet-heart sprang and laid
A muffling finger on the bell
Lest the shrill steel should strike and tell," - - 31

"And fingers touched and fancy woke," - - - 32

A Day-dream, - - - - - - - 35

ix

"For a trinket of silver, the honey-bee's moon
　Hung low in the azure, a gift from the Lord," -　-　37

Eve's Orchard, -　-　-　-　-　-　-　-　-　-　-　38

"On every royal jacket that he met
　He slashed a scarlet chevron good and strong," -　-　41

The Cypress Tree, -　-　-　-　-　-　-　44

A Glimpse of the Dome, -　-　-　-　-　46

"But broidered on his Hebrew hem
　The roses glow along," -　-　-　-　51

"In Galilee some lilies hung
　Their chalices of white," -　-　-　-　52

"A Pilgrim Flower—a troubled sea,
　A winter wild and white," -　-　-　-　-　53

"The world takes stock in Bunker Hill
　Where Freedom put the sickle in," -　-　-　-　59

"What name?" asked the preacher,
　"God knows," they said. -　-　-　-　-　63

The Light-house, -　-　-　-　-　-　-　64

"And then, as if the golden-head
　Were shaking up its feather-bed," *　-　-　-　66

"Until God's broad horizons ran,—
　The circling brotherhood of man!" -　-　-　-　68

"From Halloween to Christmas-tide!" -　-　-　-　69

'He sang. The debtor's dungeon door,
　Swung backward on its hinge of rust," -　-　-　70

"Poor Bron rhuddyn," - - - - - 71

"The post-rider of my boyhood," - - - - - 73

"The bull-dog bridges growl and growl,
  Forever at the Herald's heel," - - - - 79

"On Time!" - - - - - - - 81

"A hand has put those leaves aside,
  Lo, August Lilies light the day!" - - 85

A Mission Bell without a mission, - - - - 87

"Pour out, ye goblets, far and near,
  Your grand melodious iron flood," - - - - 89

"Ye blossoms of the furnace fires,
  Ye iron tulips rock and swing," - - - - 91

The Evening Star, - - - - - - - 94

"And then in bliss the bevy sat,
  And all in concert strangely mute,
  With roasting ears we played the flute," - - 99

A Glimpse of Spring, - - - - - - - 103

"I hear the bees' small hum-book's drone," - - - 104

"The great black cauldron bubbling slow," - - - 105

"I see a lantern boldly swinging,
  I hear its bearer bravely singing," - - - - 108

November, - - - - - - - 109

Spring Workman, - - - - - - - 112

Mt. Tamalpais, - - - - - - - 119

"Where grim Sierra shows her teeth," - - - - 120

Sequoias, - - - - - - - 121

House of Refuge, - - • - - - 123

An Offing, - • • - - - - - 124

A Farm-yard, - - - - • - - 125

Haying, - - - • • - - - - 127

Corn, - - - - - - - - - 129

"Who goes there?" - - • • - - 131

Farmers' Medallion, - - • - - - - 137

"And empty as a broken heart," • - - • - 145

The Sun-dial, - • - • - - - 148

Sweet Home, - - - - • • • - - 156

"Oh, world so utterly alone!" - - - - - 160

DULCE DOMUM.

THE SUN THAT NEVER SETS.

O N some long day of June take a terrestrial globe with all the equipments for measuring the days, the nights and the twilights; the route of the shadow and the sun; for catching Everywhere in the fine web of lines and parallels. Find Alaska whence Campbell's doleful wolf has been raising its "long howl" for a life-time. You are not looking beyond the border where floats the Flag. You have not gone from home.

Now turn the globe until Alaska is precisely at the sunset-line, then cross the continent with your fore-finger to the coast of Maine. It is sunrise and the globe has not moved at all. At the same instant closing day in Alaska, opening day in Maine, it is one country and one sun.

Of old, San Francisco was at the Western edge of this eminent domain, but now it is as far from Alaska as it is from the singing pines of our farthest East, and by this measurement in the centre of the United States. The wisdom of purchasing Alaska has been doubted, but lo, its utility is made manifest at last. It is a spot whereon the mighty sun may halt a moment just as he makes a splendid lift above the woods and fields of Maine. We hear something now and then of the British music whose

"Morning drum beats round the world."

I think it is a grander thing to say the Sun can never bid good-night to this Great Republic.

THE SUN THAT NEVER SETS.

I

PACIFIC'S waters turn to wine,
  The ripe red sun is glowing down,
With Orient pomp the gloomy pine
  Wears rubies in its plumy crown
  And shadows on its column brown.

II.

With click and stroke of slender oar
  The fishers time their homeward turn,
And pulling for Aleutian shore,
  Where dusky red the watch-fires burn,
  They trail their glittering spoils astern.

III.

I see them slide, as petrels skim
  The glassy scallops of the deep,
I hear their wild barbaric hymn
  Re-sung by pale-faced cliff and steep,
  As children sing themselves to sleep.

IV.

"Good-night" in words from loving lips,
　"Good-night, good-night," the girls reply,
"Good-night" from cañon's cold eclipse,
　"Good-night" again from skiff and sky,
　And day is dead and voices die.

V.

The flickering sea-birds seek the crag
　In dotted lines of hazy white,
The Outpost lowers the Stellar Flag
　Damp with the mists of sheeted night,
　A gray and ghostly Carmelite.

VI.

'Tis sunset on Alaska's rocks,
　Aleutian Isle and Behring's Bay,
'Tis sunrise where Atlantic shocks
　The coast of Maine in rugged play
　And domes of forest shed the day.

VII.

Sunrise in Maine! The starry wing
　Takes flight at morning gun and glow,

From tapering mast salutes the King

Whose parting foot-prints plainly show

Alaska land a breath ago

And burning yet like blood on snow.

HOW STIRS MY HEART TO THINK THIS LAND
BOUND IN LONG DAY-TIME'S YELLOW ZONE,
MAINE AND ALASKA HAND IN HAND,
THE SELF SAME HOUR BEHOLDS IN ONE
A RISING AND A SETTING SUN!

VIII.

I hear the axemen's clock-tick beat,

I hear the twang of breakfast horn,

The Yankee Doodle in the street

And Yankee Doodle in the corn;

One day not dead, another born,
Good-night is married to Good-morn!

IX.

All hail, thou Sun magnificent ;
And hail, ye Flag and Flame well met
From Orient to Occident !
These colors, O great Light, are wet
With splendors of thy golden set
And Yesterday is lingering yet.

X.

Strong as thou art and swift as strong
It takes thee thirteen hours to march
Grand Rounds from noon to noon along
The azure of the Federal arch —
Majestic sweep of boulevards,
The realm and route of traveled stars —
That spans, as rainbows span the showers,
All oaks of hearts and hopes of flowers,
As thoughts untold may thrill and throng
One mighty syllable of song.

XI.

How stirs my heart to think this Land
Bound in long day-time's yellow zone,

Maine and Alaska hand in hand,

The self-same hour beholds in one

A rising and a setting sun !

XII.

It brings my fancy to the knee

And kindles up my soul to see

Him play upon meridian lines

That string the globe as harps are strung;

To watch each fibre as it shines,

. And hear, distinct as if it rung,

The Music of the Union flung

From this celestial instrument.

Perhaps an angel choir has lent

Some Israfeel of rarest powers

To help this harper of the Lord,

And grandly sing, word after word :

This land is mine, is yours, is Ours.

THE NEW YORK "NORTH WOODS."

BORN in a wilderness that, I am glad to write, is a wilderness still, but with such clearings of loveliness and such elegancies of life as would never be sought in regions where a ride of ten miles will plunge you into forests, with the cry of panthers and the howl of wolves to wake you from your "beauty sleep"; or the leafless branches upon a lifted head in the edge of an opening to set your heart off in a gallop; or the broad tread of an oscillating bear to set the fallen leaves and limbs crackling like a hemlock fire. It is a region that has had tragedies and love-makings and adventure. It has always been a realm to me of strange mystery, startling possibility and wonderful fascination. I love its tangled trails, its tough climbs, its mighty recesses, its Druidical rocks and its endless march of woods towards Horicon and Champlain. It is not a desert because unsown, but a wilderness because everything grows and lives and does "at its own sweet will." Ah, a rare place to knit "care's ravelled sleeve," fight mosquitoes, catch fish and live a life of busy idleness.

It was in that Wonderland I first saw the weazened old printing-press. It would have done Poor Richard's heart good to ink it and work it and then order raisins and water for dinner. It is more than a century since Dr. Franklin stood up with a glass of Sparkling Delaware — water in his hand and drank "Success to printing." It was the twin of that wilderness monster the convivial spirit was toasting.

Now take the great quadruple cylinder, the mingled brains of a thousand men, that springs to the work with arms of flashing steel, that snows down sheets like flakes in Northern winter, that strikes across the continents and shines like electric light from the East even unto the West. THIS is what Dr. Franklin drank to without knowing it. A century ago indeed! It is a thousand years from press to Press.

THE NORTH WOODS.

NEW YORK, what imperial acres are these
  Where great cities in camps shed the light of their lamps
From Atlantic to Lake like a necklace of fire,

Constellations of homes shining clearer and nigher

As when star-lighted waters are stirred by the breeze.

And to think, oh, Excelsior, five millions strong

  With thy five thousand presses all playing as one,

And thy close-printed sheets flung abroad as great fleets

  Roll their clouds of white canvas and shadow the sun

That locked in thy breast like a Dorian song,

  Is a shaggy old wilderness growling with lairs

  Where the catamounts wail, and big "majors" of bears

With their plantigrade feet wipe the blackberries in,

And the lace-sifted twilights of forest begin,

  And the quick antlers lift where the quick waters drift,

And the speckled trout flash in the crystalline coid

All sprinkled with carmine and dusted with gold —

Ah, what fish but a trout could the Saviour have made

His treasurer there when the tribute was paid? —

A BIG "MAJOR" OF BEARS.

That this Dukedom of wilds could be hid in the heart

Of New York and not feel the full throb of its mart?

A PIONEER.

In that wilderness selvedge, a villager's Rest

Now empty and gone, by an orchard once stood,

Where the robins of old reared young robbers by brood,

And beyond it a house, and the charm of the place,

And as guiltless of stairs as a ground-sparrow's nest :

A mossy-browed house that was eyed like a face,

With a window each side its wide mouth of a door,

And the print of a thumb and four fingers it bore

On a panel or two, like a nobleman's crest ;

Ah, as fine and as clear as a sun-lit vignette

Is the office whence came 𝕿𝖍𝖊 𝕭𝖑𝖆𝖈𝖐 𝕽𝖎𝖛𝖊𝖗 𝕲𝖆𝖟𝖊𝖙𝖙𝖊.

AH, AS FINE AND AS CLEAR AS A SUN-LIT VIGNETTE
IS THE OFFICE WHENCE CAME THE BLACK RIVER GAZETTE.

And the editor, printer and pressman are dead,

And the "devil" withal. I have seen their low bed

    Where the Lombardies sweep the sky clear of a cloud.

As in life the one jacket could button them round,

And with one hat at once they all could be crowned,

    So in death they were laid in one coffin and shroud.

I stood in that room when a roundabout boy,

All my pockets a jumble with jewsharp and joy,

With small nibbles of sugar and fish-hooks and strings,

A new Barlow knife, alley marbles and "things,"

But my heart gave a tumble and I gave a start,

At the grim iron prince of the house of Black Art:

At the Ethiop press with one elbow a-crook,

And its rigid round arm and its sinister look,

And its hand-organ crank and its fire-dogs of legs,

And its rations of ink in a couple of kegs,

And the eagle that caught its brass claws in the thing,

And, made captive for life, could never take wing.

Tallow candles stood round, lank, languid and limp,

Too dim for an angel and too light for an imp ;

Maps of regions of darkness benighted the place

But it shone through the past with an exquisite grace.

And the boy gazed about with a silent surprise

For nothing was white but the whites of his eyes.

And the arm of the printer was dingy and long,

And the arm of the pressman was shaded and strong.

How that press came to life if I only could tell,

But who ever drew up in the bucket the star

That he saw as he leaned on the curb, in the well

When the hour was high noon and the night was afar?

Give the roller a run and the play is begun :

Up with frisket and tympan and on with the sheet,

Down with frisket and tympan in regular beat,

Then a turn at the rounce and two pulls at the bar

And the platen comes down on the face of the page

With its lines in relief like the wrinkles of age;

Then a whirl of the crank and a groan and a clank,

And the words regimental in justified rank

To a late resurrection reluctantly rise

And stand before men in their eloquent guise.

Then the sturdy-legged desk where the Editor sat

With his hand in his hair and his mail in his hat,

And the inkstand beplumed as with ferns in a fen

As if he raised geese from the slip — of the pen.

But the toil and the moil were brightened and past

For he made a man Member of Congress at last,

And honors were easy — the Member made *him.*

And he said in his heart that dipped candles were dim,

A "SPOT" IN THE WILDERNESS.

17

And he bought him a lamp, raised a "devil" to light it,
And discovered a wrong and wrote leaders to right it.
Oh, dear old Gazette, not good night but good morn,
For I hear in the twang of thy carrier's horn
The prelude to bugles right royally blown
That proclaim for the Press an estate of its own.

How my heart playing Hebrew reads back to the time
When Otsego's fair vale was a magical clime;
Not that Cooper's creations are lingering there,
But 'twas thence that my wonderful caravan came,
Books of beasts and of birds in their covers of blue —
All the rest of the pages were read through and through—
With the tiger in stripe and the leopard in star

    As if they had torn Freedom's banner in two,
And the lion bewigged like a barrister's bar,
And with H. AND E. PHINNEY's own imprint of fame.
All the s's are f's and the catch-words below
To lend me a lift as I eagerly go,
And glad as a bee in a meadow of clover
I give them a glance, wet my thumb and turn over.
More bliss blossomed out in those primers of old
Than in volumes of vellum in crimson and gold.

That imp of a press grew gigantic and grand
And startled the world as Atlantic the strand,
And I stood with bare brow by that triumph of art
When the breath was turned on and the iron-clad heart

SOME WILDERNESS WEATHER.

Of the ponderous press was beginning to beat
With the regular tramp of a troop in the street,
With the bending of springs and the flutter of wings,
And swinging of lever and swaying of bar,
    And the running of cylinders forward and back
    With a trundle of night for the letter-paved track,
With a murmur of might and a rumble and jar
And the playing of pinion and tumble of wheel
And flitter of fingers and glitter of steel,
    To and fro, up and down, over under and through,
As steady and true the magnificent iron
As the beat of chronometer timing Orion.
And I thought, with no press, without pulpit or post,
    With no English, no engine, no lightning that ran
The Celestial Express like a vanishing ghost,
    That Methuselah died when a very young man.
When the sound of the press on this wilderness broke,
And the clock was just ready to give the first stroke,
    Upon rudest of paper dead-ashen and gray
The very first words that were marshaled in print
Was "The Freeman's Own Oath." They were picking the flint
    Of young Liberty's firelock before it was day!
In this noontide, the shadows rolled up at our feet,
    And the paper dawned white as a field of fresh snow,
And the clock striking "twelve," the old Oath we repeat
    And we pass it along to the ages below.

THE CAPTAIN'S DRUM.

FRIDAY, the twenty-first of April, 1775, a horseman rode express into Enfield Street, Connecticut, with the tidings from Lexington Green. It was "Lecture day" and minister and people were in the meeting-house. Lieutenant Isaac Kibbe, the tavern-keeper who dispensed noggins of rum as befitted the times, procured drum and drummer, rudely put an end to the devotions, and Major Nathaniel Terry, a forefather of General Terry, U. S. A., led the valiant band away. The local historian reduces my Captain Abbey to the ranks.

Twenty-three years after, a child was born across the street from the meeting-house, and he dwells there yet. They had nothing against the boy as I can learn, but they gave him a Bible name that she would be a brave and reckless mother to confer upon her helpless infant in these later times, for they called him "Aholiab," and the child grew apace, furnished me with this historical incident, and has lived worthily and well "even unto this day."

How much unrecorded history, unbound and tattered pages of our national annals, is hidden away in the tills of

cedar chests, between the leaves of Family Bibles, Bunyan's
Pilgrim's Progress, Baxter's Saint's Rest, Fox's Book of Mar-
tyrs, dusty old Josephuses, antiquated old almanacs and in
feeble old memories, we shall never know. But the historic
treasure-trove that quest or chance so frequently unearths
compels the regret that the knowledge of unnumbered deeds
of virtue and of valor has utterly perished from the earth.

The great bells of centennial clocks, that during the last
ten years have been striking round the land, have done more
and better than to " make a joyful noise." They have stimu-
lated research ; they have startled multitudes with the truth
that commercial values do not attach to everything exceeding
precious ; they have quickened dead incidents ; they have
been *resurrection* bells.

THE CAPTAIN'S DRUM.

I.

IN Pilgrim land one Sabbath day
 The winter lay like sheep about
The ragged pastures mullein-gray ;
 The April sun shone in and out,
The showers swept by in fitful flocks,
And eaves ticked fast like mantel clocks.

II.

And now and then a wealthy cloud
 Would wear a ribbon broad and bright,
And now and then a winged crowd
 Of shining azure flash in sight ;
So rainbows bend and blue-birds fly
And violets show their bits of sky.

III.

To Enfield church throng all the town
 In quilted hood and bombazine,

23

In beaver hat with flaring crown

   And quaint vandyke and victorine,

And buttoned boys in roundabout

From calyx collars blossom out:

IV.

Bandanas wave their feeble fire

   And foot-stoves tinkle up the aisle,

A gray-haired Elder leads the choir

   And girls in linsey-woolsey smile.

So back to life the beings glide

Whose very graves have ebbed and died.

V.

One hundred years have waned and yet

   We call the roll, and not in vain,

For one whose flint-lock musket set

   The echoes wild round Fort Duquesne,

And swelled the battle's powder-smoke

Ere Revolution's thunders woke.

VI.

Lo, Thomas Abbey answers "Here!"

   Within the dull long-metre place;

That day upon the parson's ear
    And trampling down his words of grace
A horseman's gallop rudely beat
    Along the splashed and empty street.

VII.

The rider drew his dripping rein
    And then a letter wasp-nest gray
That ran :

*The Concord Minute Men
And red=coats had a fight to day.
To Captain Abbey this with speed.*
Ten little words to tell the deed.

VIII.

The Captain read, struck out for home
    The old quickstep of battle born,
Slung on once more a battered drum
    That bore a painted unicorn,
Then right-about, as whirls a torch
He stood before the sacred porch ; —

IX.

And then a murmuring of bees
    Broke in upon the house of prayer,

And then a wind-song swept the trees,

And then a snarl from wolfish lair,

And then a charge of grenadiers,

And then a flight of drum-beat cheers.

X.

So drum and doctrine rudely blent,

The casements rattled strange accord,

No mortal knew what either meant,

'Twas double-drag and Holy Word,

Thus saith the drum and thus the Lord.

The Captain raised so wild a rout

He drummed the congregation out !

XI.

The people gathered round amazed,

The soldier bared his head and spoke,

And every sentence burned and blazed

As trenchant as a sabre-stroke :

" 'Tis time to pick the flint to-day,

" To sling the knapsack and away —

" The Green of Lexington is red

" With British red-coats, brothers' blood !

" In rightful cause the earliest dead

" Are always best beloved of God.

'TWAS DOUBLE-DRAG AND HOLY WORD,
THUS SAITH THE DRUM AND THUS THE LORD.

"Mark time! Now let the march begin!
"All bound for Boston fall right in!"

XII.

Then *rub-a-dub* the drum jarred on,
    The throbbing roll of battle beat!
"Fall in, my men!" and one by one,
    They rhymed the tune with heart and feet,
And so they made a Sabbath march
To glory 'neath the elm-tree arch.

XIII.

The Continental line unwound
    Along the church-yard's breathless sod,
And holier grew the hallowed ground
    Where Virtue slept and Valor trod,
Two hundred strong that April day
They rallied out and marched away.

XIV

Brigaded there at Bunker Hill
    Their names are writ on Glory's page,
The brave old Captain's Sunday drill
    Has drummed its way across the Age.

HEARTS AND HEARTHS.

THERE was a time when hearths and hearts
    In rural life were counterparts —
The only neutral ground of grace
    In all this troubled world. Would I
    Could paint the homely picture right,
The low-browed dwelling's altar-place
    Forever lost, forever nigh —
Paint the divergent rays that shed
    Along the dark their lines of light
Like nimbus round a sacred head.
There, sturdy fire-dogs, legs apart,
Upheld that glowing work of art
The beech-and-maple kitchen fire,
The twinkling, crinkling, creeping fire
That gives a flash and shows a spire ;
One instant builds a phenix nest,
Another, mounts a gleaming crest,
A feu-de-joie, it shoots a jet,
Up comes a crimson minaret ;

The flame is fanned, the blaze is blown,

You hear a mill-flume's undertone —

The rattling, battling, roaring fire

With flapping flags and lapping tongues

That purrs and burrs with lion's lungs,

Expands the ring of kitchen chairs

And brightens up the brow of cares.

. The coals of rubies fall apart,

Lo, secrets of a burning heart :

The embers show a Valentine,

Dead faces smile, lost castles shine

And pansies blow and eglantine,

And old gold beads and rings of price

And buds and birds of Paradise.

A soft red twilight charms the room

And fills it like a faint perfume.

There, couples sat the night away

Whist as a button-hole bouquet —

Some russets roasting in a row,

Some talking flames that "told of snow,"

Some cider that her hands had drawn,

Two pairs of lips, a single cup,

Both kissed the brim and drank it up.

The candle has its night-cap on,

FOR UP THE SWEETHEART SPRANG, AND LAID

A MUFFLING FINGER ON THE BELL

LEST THE SHRILL STEEL SHOULD STRIKE AND TELL.

The very embers gone to bed —

Who shall record what either said?

Or who so eloquent can tell

How early apples used to smell?

The woodsy, evanescent taste

Of berries plucked with eager haste

AND FINGERS TOUCHED AND FANCY WOKE —

As through the meadow lands they crept,

And fingers touched and fancy woke

And never slumbered, never slept

'Till Day on life's sweet dreamings broke?

The pious clock a murmur made,

    Held up both hands before its face,

        Not meant so much for twelve o'clock

        But just astonishment and shock

    At such a want of modest grace,

For up the sweetheart sprang and laid

    A muffling finger on the bell

Lest the shrill steel should strike and tell,

And gave the hands a backward whirl,

Took time "on tick," the reckless girl !

Where is the lover ?   Old and lone.

And where the maiden ?   Gray and gone.

I read the dim *Italic* stone :

    A willow tree, a " Sacred To "—

The sad old story ever new,

For all the twain the world moves on.

I saw a spider drift about

    Upon the sun-shot morning air,

        As if like thistle blossoms blown

        At random, desolate and strown,

    Now here and there and everywhere,

And all the while that aeronaut

Was paying nature's life-line out !

I traced it by the nervous thread

Back to its little silken lair

Safe hid in a verbena bed.

It never cut that cable fine

But felt its home along the line.

And then I thought, and then I said

Our life-line is the love of home,

Oh, make it fast where'er you roam —

Amid the rough world's rolling strife

It is the anchorage· of life.

A LAMENT FOR ADAM.

I AM always bewailing the desolate fate
   Of the primal old Crusoe who led off the race
With no boots and no boyhood, no swing on the gate,
   What could Paradise be with its garden of grace

A DAY DREAM.

35

To a being who never had felt himself grow

But had stood up and lived like the Parian snow

At the touch of the sculptor ?   Lone Nobody's son

With a world to himself and a census of one.

Lo, a man with no story to linger behind,

If we only except the Darwinian kind —

Lo, an orphan by birth though no creature had died,

Or been born, wooed or wed as bridegroom or bride.

I look up the gray eons with wondering thought

   Where humanity's Duke in his nakedness strode,

All uncrowned and untraveled, unlettered, untaught,

   With no fire but the sun and the lair for abode.

Not a word could he write, not a breath could he read,

It was Adam, "*his*. X *mark*," to the lease and the deed.

Ah, the hermit of Eden could never have dreamt

   That his boys would wear pinions forever unfurled

   And away down the line would track up the round world

With their highways and thoughtways, as a comet unkempt,

A fourth Fury of fire by Omnipotence driven,

Dishevels her hair on the bosom of Heaven ;

Would have turnpiked the planet and graded the sky,

Swept meridian lines in the glance of an eye

With their flashes of lightning and footprints of ink,

Till the lumbering globe was beginning to think !

The world was all ready for bridegroom and bride

When Adam awoke from his wonderful swoon
And Creation's fair crown lay alive by his side;
For a trinket of silver, the honey-bee's moon
Hung low in the azure, a gift from the Lord,
For her garments, bright emerald garnished the trees,
And her flounces and aprons slow swung in the breeze,

And the violets caught her blue glance from the sward;
With the flush of new life she just lifted her head
And the roses of York blushed a Lancaster red,
And the whispers ran round like the rustle of leaves
And the young woods of Paradise laughed in their sleeves.

Now Eden to Earth doth this legacy leave:
The month of that wedding of emerald ray
Shall wear through the cycles the colors of Eve,
Shall belong to all ages forever and aye,
With its birds in full song and its breezes in tune,
So she left her best clothes to Magnificent June.

EVE'S ORCHARD.

"DON'T GIVE UP THE SHIP."

ONE hundred years ago this blesséd day
   The schooner Franklin grounded on a bar,
And British boats swarmed down upon the prey
   As thick as bees where clover blossoms are.
She was a fighting schooner, and the sky
   Was clouded up with battle near and far,
And like a flame the crimson flag did fly—
She had her choice to strike it or to die.
They took the hapless schooner fore and aft,
With whips of living fire they lashed the craft,
'Twas raining iron and 'twas lightening steel,
   And cannon thundered through the heavy weather,
'Twas crash and flash—'twas shout and whirl and wheel,
And splintered fire and muskets' rattling peal,
   And cheers and curses went aloft together
Redder than sunset was the Franklin's deck,
And many a sea-dog lay a shattered wreck.

They brought the ship about until she wore
Nearer hell's port than she had sailed before.

The schooner's Captain bore an unknown name
    That never had been heard in song or story,
And yet the gallant WINGFORD's heart of flame
    Should light a ballad of Centennial glory.
One hundred years ago this day he died,
One hundred years ago this day he cried
Amid the throe and tempest of despair,
" The FLAG, my men, we'll keep it floating there !"

Splashed like a wine-press, wounded, sore-beset,
    Swath after swath he cut right through the throng,
On every royal jacket that he met
    He slashed a scarlet chevron good and strong ;
He cleared a place to die with swinging stroke,
His cutlass clanged upon the slippery oak,
He fell, and gave one upward lightning glance
That shone an instant like the flash of lance,
For there aloft the fiery flag yet swung
And lapped the murky cloud, a crimson tongue —
He rallied up his soul and voice and cried
" Oh, don't give up the ship !" and so he died

ON EVERY ROYAL JACKET THAT HE MET,
HE SLASHED A SCARLET CHEVRON GOOD AND STRONG.

If that *be* dying, and the sailors heard
And took the Captain at his latest word.

Great Heart, good-night! Death made thee commodore.
And yet no orders for an hundred years!
Why name this man a century ashore?
  I'll tell you why. They could have spared their tears
Who mourned him dead. He is not dead at all,
He was not made to smother in a pall.
Men are alive who might have heard him speak
Amid the thunders of the Chesapeake
Those very accents, "don't give up the ship!"
That rang again from Lawrence' dying lip.

By some new name here, there and everywhere,
The soul of courage breathes the living air.
One noble deed may bless the race, and when,
As myriads now asleep, men die for men
And Liberty and God, the deed inspires
And kindles and exults like prairie fires,
  Until, horizon to horizon broad,
It makes day's camp-fire in an utter night
And doubles noon-time to intenser light.
  It wilts the flowers indeed and glooms the sod,

But one sweet May will end the sad eclipse

And flowers will worship with their scarlet lips

 And lilies pray and make all right with God.

And so our vast encampments of the Blue

 May have their marching orders any day,

And pass the world again in grand review,

 Defend the right and hold the wrong at bay —

May haunt with valor some poor halting heart

Till seeming clods to instant manhood start,

Cast off, as lightnings flash, their long disguise

And stand transfigured to our earnest eyes.

LINCOLN AND HIS PSALM.

TO lay hands upon Lincoln's classic text for any sake may be presumption, but, in my desire to show how near akin are the Maker, who is the poet, and the Doer, I have been guilty of this thing. Whoever rises to the dignity of great truth or grand achievement, a solemn earnestness shed upon him like a glory out of Heaven, is so much a poet that, without his knowledge, his words strike into the stately Epic march or spring away in Lyric flight.

And so, by jostling a word here and there out of its rightful place in the compact line, the utterances of the poetic soul are easily adjusted to poetic semblance. The grandest moods in men, like the royal scenes in nature, where each grows salient as if it would touch the Heavens, are never merry. There is no laughter in the Mountain that robed in the ermine of immortal winters stands up to judge the World. But the brook at his foot idles on with a childish laugh and is forgotten.

To me, Lincoln's strong and rugged face was always a poem in itself. There were flashes of wit and flickers of

humor like glimpses of sunshine in a shady place, but ever
in those kind and gentle eyes an unspeakable sadness, as if,
no matter what the lips were saying, they were always seeing
the mission of their master's life, at once an anthem and a
dirge, that should touch unreckoned ages, and make his
words imperishable as our English speech.

Ah, "it is a dread and awful thing to" *live* so grand a
life as it is to die a tragic death.

LINCOLN AND HIS PSALM.

DECORATION DAY.

MOVE on, ye pilgrims to the Springfield tomb —
    Be proud to-day, O portico of gloom,
Where lies the man in solitary state
    Who never caused a tear but when he died
        And set the flags around the world half-mast.
The gentle Tribune and so grandly great
That e'en the utter avarice of Death
        That claims the world, and will not be denied,
Could only rob him of his mortal breath.
            How strange the splendor though the man be past!
            His noblest inspiration was his last.
    The statues of the Capitol are there
        As when he stood upon the marble stair
    And said those words so tender, true and just,
    A royal psalm that took mankind on trust —
Those words that will endure and he in them
While May wears flowers upon her broidered hem
        And all that marble snows and drifts to dust:

"FONDLY do we hope, fervently we pray,

"That this mighty scourge of war may speedily pass away;

"With charity for all, with malice toward none,

  "With firmness in the right

  "As God shall give us light,

"Let us finish the work already begun —

"Care for the battle sons, the Nation's wounds to bind,

"Care for the helpless ones that they will leave behind,

"Cherish it we will, achieve it if we can,

"A just and lasting peace forever unto Man!"

Amid old Europe's rude and thundering years

  When peoples strove as battle-clouds are driven,

One calm white angel of a day appears

  In every year, a gift direct from Heaven,

Wherein from setting sun to setting sun

No thought or deed of bitterness was done.

  "Day of the truce of God!" Be this day ours

    Until perpetual peace flows like a river,

    And hopes as fragrant as the tribute flowers

    Fill all the land forever and forever.

THE TWO ARMIES.

O NE bright September day I rode
Through prairie sweeps horizon-broad,
And saw a host a million strong
Drawn up in columns dense and long,
All silken-tasseled and beplumed.
No bugle blew, no cannon boomed,
No orders rang along the lines
But whispers as in woods of pines.
They stood erect in bright array
And filled the splendid eye of day.

Nine English miles from front to flank,
Nine English miles from wing to wing,
And as I flew from rank to rank
They came about with stately swing.
What hosts are these that wave the sword?
And quick returned the answering word,
"One Standing Army of the Lord!

The emerald regiments of corn
At reveillé salute the morn !

Now open out, ye legions green !
Let strange battalions march between
Up to the front as they were wont,
Ay, let the azure squadrons through,
A grander armament than you,
Two hundred thousand Boys in Blue !
The nation's graves have ebbed away
And blent in dust the blue and gray.
All peaceful as a field of maize,
No billowed flags nor battle's blaze ;
Thank God for calm from pine to palm,
Strike up the benediction psalm :
Now unto God be all the praise,
To Blue and Gray good morn ! good night !
With one accord strike hands for right,
And one the glory and the sheen,
We'll fight new battles in the green !

ROSE, LILY,
AND MAY FLOWER.

I.

IN Sharon's Vale some roses grew
Three thousand years ago,
And bloomed their little season through,
And shed their leaves when winter blew
Like flakes of fragrant snow.

II.

A royal hand did gather them
And set them in his Song,
You cannot find his diadem
But broidered on his Hebrew hem
The roses glow along.

III.

The stately Ages tread aside
Where'er those roses are,

Though realms have vanished,
diamonds died,
Old Sharon's children yet abide
As deathless as a star.

CHRIST'S LILIES

I.

In Galilee some lilies hung
　Their chalices of white,
And to and fro their fragrance flung,
So many cups of incense swung
　Before the Lord of light.

II.

The Turk and Christian trod to death
　The glory of the shrine,
And left no lily's grave beneath
Nor speechless eloquence of breath
　To sweeten Palestine.

III.

These idle princes of their race
　Have never died at all;

Behold them in Judean grace

As rallied round a holier place

    Within his instant call,

IV.

They smile and wait at God's right hand

    And grow of strange account,

For angels watch them as they stand

Amid that lily-garden land,

    The Sermon on the Mount.

THE MAY FLOWER.

I.

    A Pilgrim Flower—a troubled sea,

    A winter wild and white,

    Its only world was on the lea,

    A tempest caught and swept it free

    To wilderness and night.

II.

Oh, Christians, for the May Flower pray,
    Each petal is a soul!
Adrift and doomed this Flower of May,
Oh, women, weep your hearts away,
    Oh, gray-haired Sexton, toll!

III.

December waited gaunt and grim
    Within its lair of snow,
The shaggy forests ghostly dim
Stood up and sang a funeral hymn
    Two hundred years ago.

IV.

‚That stranded flower was strangely blent
    Of amaranth and May;
From marble tower to miner's tent,
Where'er the Anglo-Saxon went
    It brightens night and day.

V.

Oh, roses, lilies, flowers of May!
    Akin to human kind,
The Ages bear ye on their way —
Bound in one sweet and rare bouquet
    An endless Spring is twined.

MASSACHUSETTS SENDS GREETING.

I MET a man away down East
Who towered amid the eight-rowed corn
Raccoons could finish at a feast,
    And listened for the dinner-horn.
A crow aloft on a hemlock limb
Looked black at what would fall to him.
The bilious earth lay blank beneath,
His angry hoe showed signs of teeth,
So nicked and notched with glance and glint
At bowlder gray and sparkling flint.
He saw a pumpkin's yellow blow
And touched it with his thoughtful toe,
Prophetic flower of by-and-by,
Forerunner of one pumpkin pie!

"Out West? Jes' so! From Illinoi?
"My Jem is there — my oldest boy —
"And John's in Kansas, so is Jane,
"She married one Elnathan Payne ; —

"And mother too — *she* wants to go .

"No musket ever scattered so ;

"And then it allus p'ints one way —

"Right where them big per-aries lay.

"Betwixt them two — Death and the West —

"They git our youngest, strongest, best.

"It's queer the grave-yard keeps a-growin'

"As ef nobody dreamed of goin'!

"It's there right where them brooms o' trees

"Are sweepin' *nothin'* in the breeze.

"A queen-bee in an empty hive

"Is all o' mine that's left alive.

"I call them *dead* I never see,

"The West or Heaven's all one to me —

"I wait an' wait — God give me grace!

"They don't come back from *either* place.

"Them miles an' miles of level land,

"And ev'ry tree brought up by hand,

"The sky shut down around the green

"As snug as any soup-tureen.

"Poor show for David with his sling

"An' not a pebble fit to fling."

So talked the Massachusetts man
And paused for breath and then began :
"I hear you have," the farmer said,
"A creature with a horse's head,
  "A cricket's body, dragon's wings,
"The long hind legs of a kangaroo,
  "The hungriest of created things
"That eats a landskip through an' through ;
  "A boarding-house for bugs may be
  "The place for you but not for me."

Alas, old man, I sadly said,
They are, indeed, most nobly fed ;
You taunt us with no dainty touch,
  But had those creatures boarded *here*
  It would have saved us many a fear,
They could not harm you very much,
  And then it cannot be denied,
  They surely would have starved and died.

"I wouldn't swap the old Bay State,"
The farmer cried with voice elate,—
He stood upright in every joint
As any exclamation-point,

And hoe and stone struck instant fire

As if he thus touched off his ire,—

" I wouldn't swap the old Bay State,

" It's rugged rocks and mountains great,

" For land as level as a hone,

" All ready fenced and seeded down.

" Our grain stands slender in the shock,

   " The grists are light we send to mill,

" But then we gave you Plymouth Rock

      " Where Freedom's clearins' first begin ;

    " The world takes *stock* in Bunker Hill,

    " Where Freedom put the sickle in.

" You've Injuns West but we're ahead,

" Our Boston Mohawks allus led,

" That took a cargo of Bohea

" An' steeped a drawin' in the sea

" An' asked young Liberty to tea !

" They snuff at Boston, and they dub

" The good old town the Yankee 'Hub.'

" What all it means I never knew,

" *My* way at least, it may be true :

" I know its gritty boys go out

   " Like spokes of wheels to reach the rim

" That binds creation all about

"THE WORLD TAKES STOCK IN BUNKER HILL
"WHERE FREEDOM PUT THE SICKLE IN."

"Till West an' East an' South an' North,

   "You hear their whistle or their hymn

"Around the felly of the earth!"

The old man heard the dinner-horn

And stumped away among the corn.

The truth had lighted up his face

And lent the furrowed features grace.

He turned and called across the lot,

"There's one thing more I 'most forgot;

"Ef you *see* Jem or John or Jane,

    "Jes' tell 'em where you've been to-day;

"That I yit walk the narrow lane

"Whose end is growin' mighty plain,

    "And that I send 'em far away

"One word from Massachusetts sod,

"The blessin' of their Fathers' God,

   And tell 'em too, an Eastern boy

"Must make a *man* in Illinoi."

Such hearty, homely words he spoke,

The chimney wore a plume of smoke,

The wife stood watching at the door,

Good-by, old man, forevermore.

"GOD KNOWS."

I.

AN emigrant ship with a world aboard
Went down by the head on the Kentish coast,
No tatter of bunting at half-mast lowered,
No cannon to toll for the creatures lost.
Two hundred and twenty their souls let slip,
Two hundred and twenty with speechless lip
Went staggering down in the foundered ship.

II.

Nobody can tell it — nor you nor I,
The frenzy of fright when lightning thought
Wove like a shuttle the far and nigh,
Shot quivering streams through the long forgot,
And lighted the years with a ghastly glare,
A second a year, and a second to spare,
'Mid surges of water and gasps of prayer.

III.

The heavens were doom and the Lord was dumb,
The cloud and the breaker were blent in one,

No angel in sight, not any to come!

God pardon their sins for the Christ His Son!

The tempest died down as the tempest will,

The sea in a rivulet drowse lay still,

The roses were red on the rugged hill —

The roses that blow in the early light

And die into gray with the mists of night.

IV.

Then drifted ashore in a night-gown dressed

    A waif of a girl with her sanded hair,

And hands like a prayer on her cold blue breast,

    And a smile on her mouth that was not despair.

No stitch on the garment ever to tell

Who bore her, who lost her, who loved her well,

Unnamed as a rose — was it Norah or Nell?

V.

The coasters and wreckers around her stood,

    And gazed on the treasure-trove landward cast,

As round a dead robin the sturdy wood,

    Its plumage all rent and the whirlwind past.

They laid a white cross on her home-made vest,

The coffin was rude as a red-breast's nest,

And poor was the shroud, but a perfect rest

Fell down on the child like dew on the West.

VI.

A ripple of sod just covered her over,

Nobody to bid her "good-night, my bird!"

Spring waited to weave a quilt of red clover,

Nobody alive had her pet name heard.

"WHAT NAME?" ASKED THE PREACHER,
"GOD KNOWS!" THEY SAID

"What name?" asked the preacher, "God knows!" they said.

Nor waited nor wept as they made her bed,

But sculptured "God knows" on the slate at her head.

VII.

The lesson be ours when the night runs wild,

The road out of sight and the stars gone home,

Lost hope or lost heart, lost Pleiad or child,

Remember the words at the drowned girl's tomb.

Bewildered and blind the soul can repose

Whether cypress or laurel blossoms and blows,

Whatever betides for the good "God knows"—

God knows all the while—our blindness His sight,

Our darkness His day, our weakness His might.

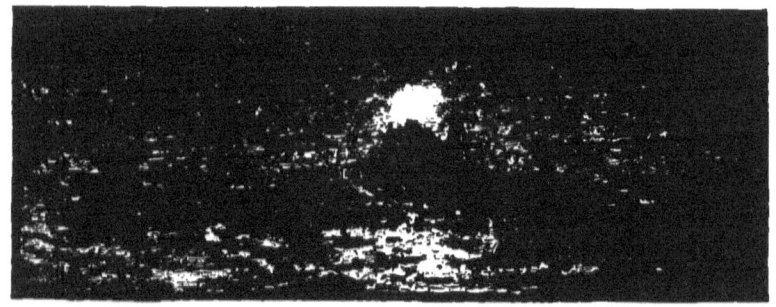

THISTLE SERMON.

PRAY let the gaudy tulip go
       For Scotland's flower with crimson crest,
That wears a bee on every blow
    And bristles like a bandit dressed ;
That drifts its silver life-balloon
Along the year's dull afternoon
Bound for another Spring, and girds
The feeble heart like holy words.

Just as the seeds are fit to fly
    A yellow-bird drops deftly down,
A living nugget from the sky,
    And lights upon the thistle brown.
And then, as if the golden-head
Were shaking up its feather bed,
A little breathless tempest breaks
About the bird in silver flakes,
A cunning cloud of flock and fleck —
Alas, the thistle is a wreck !

But no, the seeds are taking wing,

The goldfinch has no time to sing

For taking toll, and then the gale

Sweeps out the fleet of silk and sail,

AND THEN, AS IF THE GOLDEN-HEAD
WERE SHAKING UP ITS FEATHER BED.

And so, the weeds are always here,

And finches dine another year,

And so, O troubled Soul, good cheer!

A BIRTH-DAY.

DECEMBER 17TH. 1807.

I.

NEW ENGLAND bred, December born,
 Oh, eldest son of Doric song,
We bid thy fame and thee good morn!
 The welcomes of the world belong
To thee. Thanksgiving Day drifts down
To set thy birth-right in its crown.

II.

Thanks for thy bugle-horn that played
 Oppression's Dead March round the land,
Thanks for thy ringing harp that made
 New pulses leap in Labor's hand,
Thanks for thy trumpet's Gabriel blast
That rallied out the right at last.

III.

Thanks for thy psaltery's iron strings
 That shook their rhythmic thunders out

As eagles spurn with clashing wings

   The mountain eyrie's rock redoubt,

Until God's broad horizons ran

The circling brotherhood of man !

IV.

Thanks for thy golden bees that hum

   The fragrant tunes of summer through

The year ; forever go and come

   With all things sweet and pure and true,

And lend these dull and daily lives

The music of the murmuring hives.

V.

Midway between Thanksgiving Day

   And Christmas Eve a cradle rocked,

An angel left his radiant way

   And stood beside the door and knocked.

Before him waved the Christmas glow,
Behind him whirled the drifting snow.

VI.

The door swung wide. Beyond his feet
    The yule-log streamed a golden light,
As if a small celestial street
    Were ribbon'd on the breast of night
Let grace and mercy here abide
From Halloween to Christmas-tide!

VII.

"Now peace on earth," the angel said,
    "Praise God the Father and the Son,"
And so above that infant head
    The carol and the psalm begun,
Translated since in every tongue,
By battle thundered, Mercy sung.

VIII.

The Christmas coal that touched his lips,
    The Christmas soul that warmed his breast,
Unquenched to-day in earth's eclipse
    Is yet aglow, is still a guest,—
In roll of timbrel, song of wren,
'Tis " peace on earth, good will to men ! "

IX

He sang. The debtor's dungeon door
    Swung backward on its hinge of rust,
The chains clanked down that bondmen wore
    And blood cried out from speechless dust,
Till skies of daisies starred the sod
Where terror knelt and tyrant trod.

X.

He sang. And poor Bron rhuddyn's throat
  Was trembling sweet with English song.
He sang. And bolted lightnings smote
  The grizzly battlements of Wrong.
Strike not thy "Tent" beside the sea,
Brave Laureate of Liberty!

XI.

Not "Snow-bound" yet, this later John
  Sings Eden's dear old songs again,
And WHITTIER'S Pilgrims travel on
  Till Time's last anthem sounds AMEN.

ROCK EYRIE.

WHERE mountains lift forever at high tide,
Where air is crystal and the near stars ride,
Empyreal Admirals of the Blue,
And silver snow-drifts mock the silver true,
'Mid Nature's high relief, Rock Eyrie, hail!

Oh, friend afar, could prayer of mine avail
Thy cloudless soul should match thy cloudless skies,
Crowned with all joy thy DULCE DOMUM rise,
Be every day good-morning and good-night,
Till dawn celestial brings the perfect light.

See Frontispiece.

72

THE FLYING HERALDS.

I CAN see him now — the post-rider of my boyhood, in his muskrat cap, and his overcoat with half as many capes as North America; his thin section of a horse that trotted on one leg and cantered with the other three. I can hear his tin horn, like the buzz of an unamiable bee, as he summoned the people out to gate or bars for the damp dry Weekly poor Desdemona could cover with her handkerchief.

Afterward, I rode on the Fast White Mail that whirled a hundred tons of print and pen a thousand miles a day, and halted the sun that it should not go down until the morning paper of New York had been read in "the land of the Beautiful River." All the whips and spurs of Derby Day were as the lazy click of a grandam's needles slow knitting by the kitchen fire, to that wild rattling ride, and when the miles grew short and shorter still, it was like a flight of ringing cheers. Swiftest motion is intensest life

THE FLYING HERALDS.

SLING up the bugle! Harp and lute,
   Let every dusty string be mute.
Be still the drum and dumb the flute,
While trumpets blow so brave and loud
   They rally like a flag unfurled
   And wake and warm the startled world —
The trumpets of the " Flying Cloud."
That silver breath of steam adrift
   As lazy as a morning mist,
Can whirl an engine winged and swift
As whirls a fan's small ounce of lift
   At the turn of my lady's wrist -
Can stitch this planet's raveled robe,
Gird like a slender girl the globe
Till far-off cities meet and mate
As neighbors gossip at the gate.
Lo, there the Eagle Chariots come!
The gorges growl, the bridges drum,
The tunneled thunder rumbles grum.

A blast of trumpet long and loud,

Black clouds for pall and white for shroud,

And starry sparkles raining fast,

As if, God's autumn come at last,

I saw adrift and tempest-rent

A tatter of the firmament.

"FIFTY MINUTES LATE."

Pull out, my gallant engineer!

Take aim along the smooth air line,

The way is clear, the far is near,

Five hundred miles and then we dine.

Upon Chicago draw a bead —

See where she lifts her antlered head,

Her masted fleets like woods of pine.

With clash and clank and roar and ring

And clang of bell and trumpet blare

And comet head-light's growing glare

Old Vulcan's self has taken wing!

With rattling rock and swinging swerves

He fearless sweeps the splendid curves,

Lies over to the nervous work

As wheel the chargers of the Turk.

The engineer whips out his watch —

The train is fifty minutes late!

"Old Time's a nimble thing to catch,"

He says, "but then I'm sure as fate,

"Shove in the diamonds there, my mate!"

The mile-posts glitter like a grate.

The red-mouth'd furnace yawns for more

And gives a husky, hungry roar,

It shakes a thunder-cloud of mane

Above the quiver of the train,

Down comes the lever quick and strong,

The Eagle Chariots plunge along.

'Tis whip and spur and rail and steel,

'Tis flash and rush and rock and reel

As if one streak of early dawn

Should travel night-time and be gone.

See all the while the driver stand,

His heart-beat in his bridle hand,

His hair by gusty night blown back —

It blows whene'er *he* has the track ;

His eye is on the iron bars

That swing around to let him through,

He hums a tune and thanks his stars

"The Lansing's" stanch and tried and true.

His brow is wet with mental sweat,

He says, "I'm sure to make it yet —

"My grand old lady does her best."

His soul is in the distant West,

His watch is burning in his vest.

Its bloodless hands that mock the dead

    Wipe off the minutes from its face

As if the tears that Time had shed

    For some lost hope or perished grace.

What if a paltry breath of space

Would save that "foot-board" hero there

    His well-earned knighthood of the road,

Those hands would never heed the prayer

    But mark the fatal hour he owed.

The frantic bell is on the ring,

The furnace door is on the swing,

The Fast White Mail is on the wing.

It whistles up the stealthy roads

    That creep across the iron way,

It brightens up the still abodes

    Of them that weep or sleep or pray.

The mighty eye glares down the rails,

The cruel wheels come down like flails,

The bull-dog bridges growl and growl

    Forever at the Herald's heel,

The mile-posts all are cheek by jowl

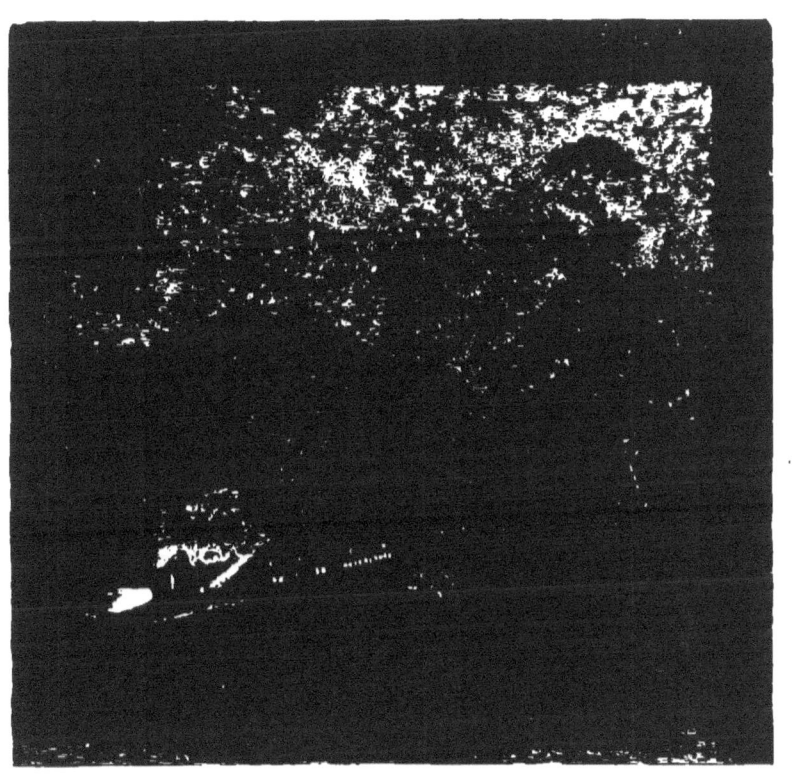

THE BULL-DOG BRIDGES GROWL AND GROWL
FOREVER AT THE HERALD'S HEEL.

And sixty in an hour!

It means far more than steam and steel,

This wondrous burst of pinion power,

Means tempered grit and iron will,

Means nerve and faith and brain and skill.

"TWENTY MINUTES LATE."

The twain at last have struck their gait —

The engine and the engineer.

"The train is twenty minutes late!"

The smutty fireman gives a cheer.

He lets her out in giant strides,

She thrusts her slender arms of steel

Deep in the caskets at her sides,

The nervous creature seems to feel

For something precious hidden there;

Plucks out great handfuls of the power

That gives her sixty miles an hour,

And flings and tosses everywhere

Huge volumes of the power asleep,

As if a thousand fleecy sheep

Turned out to pasture in the air.

"She buckles bully to the work,

"She's not the kind of girl to shirk,"

The driver says, and tries the gauge

And never dreams he leads the age.

Full seventy feet at a single plunge,

And seventy feet at a single breath,

And seventy feet from instant death !

A little slower than the lunge

The lightning makes that stabs the night,

And faster than a falcon's flight.

'Tis seventy feet at every beat

Of heart and clock the train is hurled,

At such a rate with such a mate

Not eighteen days around the world.

"ON TIME !"

The hamlets scatter from the path,

As tempests blow the aftermath,

. And wild as deer the woods retreat

That met and whispered in the street.

"Down brakes ! A haystack blocks the route !"

And there ! It slowly waltzes out.

A mighty shadow inks the track

    As if a mountain should lie down

    And leave the print from foot to crown —

Before you think it there and back

    We cut the shadow through and through,

The telegraphic poles grow dense

    As forests of the tall bamboo,

That swift striped streak is just a fence

    As if ten miles of ribbon flew.

'Tis neck and neck. The driver smiles,

He's running down the missing miles.

The train swims on with easy sway

    As supple as a serpent's glide,

Chicago and the break of day

    And miles and minutes side by side !

White lights and red, green lights and blue,

The thorough-breds have pulled us through —

Through snow and blow and ray and rack,

    A thousand miles ! One night and day !

From black to white, from white to black.

    " My move," I hear the driver say,

" Checkmate to Time ! We've won the game,

" The race for life, the flight for fame —

" Chicago ! and we kept the track."

AUGUST LILIES.

D IED last night at twelve o'clock
The richest month of all the year
Her belted grain in sheaf and shock
Like gold encampments far and near.

The rose-tree mourns in spider's crape,
At half-mast stands the hollyhock,
The rock that five-leaved ivies drape
Has dared to rob some prince of Tyre
And wear his robe of purple fire.

The lively locust's rattling watch
Is always busy running down,
The cricket sings its breathless catch
And sunflowers lift the yellow crown.
As if a fairies' grave-yard lent
Its slender bones to dance a match,
Cicadæ's knees and elbows bent,

In flurries whirl, a crazy set,
To click of Moorish castanet.

III.

Unto this August, Time has told
　　Down thirty perfect days in rhyme,
Unsullied hours a minute old,
　　A minute from celestial clime,
　　With two full moons to shine the while,
Twelve hours were silver, twelve were gold ;
　　Five Sabbath mornings' peaceful smile
To light the radiant weeks along,
With flush of leaf and flights of song.

IV.

O Queen of Months, a splendid dower
　　Was thine, and yet thou could'st not wait
For all this wealth one little hour
　　But met inevitable fate !
　　Broad leaves have hid all summer long
　　A precious thing beside my gate.
　　One after one each floral throng
Had perished, but those leaves still kept
Their secret as if something slept.

A HAND HAS PUT THOSE LEAVES ASIDE,
LO, AUGUST LILIES LIGHT THE DAY!
SO FAIR, AS IF SOME ANGEL DIED
AND TOOK THIS MONUMENTAL WAY.

V.

A hand has put those leaves aside,

Lo, August Lilies light the day!

So fair, as if some angel died

And took this monumental way;

So pure, as if some Singer sweet

Had touched it with her lips and sighed

Because these chaliced lives so fleet,

These dear Day Lilies, only last

While each swift day is going past.

And yet why not? Why tarry here

Till dark and drear November comes

To play the Dead March on its drums

Of sleet, and freeze the falling tear.

CENTENNIAL BELLS.

HAVING written a poem I made a pilgrimage to Independence Hall to see the subject. It was a delight to find the awkward wound has never healed; that the gloomy dome is dingy; older than the Republic but with a refresh-

A DUMB BELL.

ing suspicion of greenness. The sacred text is there yet; the first proclamation of liberty, that in the Old Testament is a command, but transferred to the Old Bell was a prophecy. The iron preacher pounded and expounded from that verse and stuck to the text as nobody else has, since Paul stood on Mars Hill. There are old Mission Bells a-many that are dumb, but Independence Hall has a Bell with a Mission, and so it can never be hushed.

I put the old man in the belfry and gave him white hair and made him as glad and as mad as he could live; and I set the boy on the stairs to call out to the ringer when the signing was done, and presented the lad with a pair of blue eyes because it is a fast color and I liked him; and yet I knew all the while that the Magi of the West, who are the Paul Prys of mankind and "disturbers of the peace" of the quick and the dead, declare the old man had no more idea for what he was ringing than the bell-wether of a flock of sheep, and that there was no such boy on the stairs nor any boy at all. If the incident is a fiction it is a melancholy pity, for it ought to be a fact.

CENTENNIAL BELLS.

Y E belfry'd blacksmiths in the air,
  Smite your sweet anvils good and strong!
Ye lions in your lofty lair
  Roar out from tower to tower along
The wrinkled coasts and scalloped seas
Till winter meet the orange breeze

POUR OUT, YE GOBLETS, FAR AND NEAR,
YOUR GRAND MELODIOUS IRON FLOOD.

89

From bridal lands that always wear
The blesséd blossoms round their hair.
Centennial Bells, ring on !

Pour out, ye goblets, far and near,
  Your grand melodious iron flood,
Till pine and palm shall think they hear
  The axes smite the stately wood,
Nor dream the measured cadence meant
The clock-tick of the Continent,
The foot-fall of a world that nears
The field-day of a hundred years.

Ye blossoms of the furnace fires,
  Ye iron tulips rock and swing.
The people's primal age expires,
  One hundred years the reigning king.
Strike " one," ye hammers overhead,
Ye rusty tongues, ring off the red,
Ring up the Concord Minute Men,
Ring out old Putnam's wolf again.

Ring down the curtain on To-day
And give the Past the right of way,
Till fields of battle red with rust
Shine through the ashes and the dust

Across the Age, and burn as plain
As glowing Mars through window-pane —
How grandly loom like grenadiers
These heroes with their hundred years!

YE BLOSSOMS OF THE FURNACE FIRES,
YE IRON TULIPS ROCK AND SWING.

Ring for the blue-eyed errand-boy
That quavered up the belfry stair,
"They've signed it! Signed it!" and the joy
Rolled forth as rolls the Delaware.
The old man started from a dream,
His white hair blew, a silver stream,
Above his head the bell unswung
Dumb as a morning-glory hung;
The time had come awaited long,
His wrinkled hand grew young and strong.

He grasped the rope as men that drown
Clutch at the life-line drifting down,
The iron dome as wildly flung
As if Alaska's winds had rung.

Strange that the founder never knew
When from the molten glow he drew
That bell, he hid within its rim
An anthem and a birth-day hymn.

So rashly rung, so madly tossed,
Its old melodious volume lost,
Its thrilled horizon rent and cleft,
Of sweet vibration all bereft,
And yet to hear that tocsin break
The silence of a hundred years,
Its rude discordant murmurs shake
And rally out the soul in cheers
Would set me longing to be rid
Of sweeter voices and to bid
    Centennial Bells be dumb.

Although no mighty Muscovite,
    No iron welkin rudely hurled,
That bell of Liberty and Right
    Was heard around the Babel world.

Land of the green and golden robe,

   A three hours' journey for the Sun,

Two oceans kiss thee round the globe,

   Up the steep earth thy rivers run

From geologic ice to June,

A hundred years from night to noon.

   In blossom still like Aaron's rod,

The clocks are on the stroke of one —

   One land, one tongue, one flag, one God !

   Centennial Bells, ring on !

TWO RIVERS AND TWO SHIPS.

W HEN certain people say of a man "he is sentimental,"
they mean to pluck out his beard and make a finish
of his manhood; of a woman, that she is an amiable fool.
The stout world sometimes fears anything tender but "legal
tender," steaks and muffins. In cultivating hard heads on
their shoulders men come to carry trilobites in their left
breasts. As a rule, all childhood shrinks instinctively from
him who forgets or despises his own, and he who will not
confess to a soft place in his heart is quite sure to have one
in his head.

Of all earthly charms there is none so ineffable and exquisite as the charm of youth. It invests indifferent things
with a grace that is almost beauty. That it must perish
like a vanishing vision at dawning day, has been a burden
of lament with the manliest of men. A love for creeping
back under the world's Eastern eaves, and being for a moment "the father of the man" again, is almost as restful
and inspiring as a view from Bunyan's Delectable Mountains whence the Celestial City is in sight.

These paragraphs are written as a placard of warning, a sort of " Beware," to those who would have nobody know they were ever ten-toed boys, lest they may blunder upon poetical premises with so much that breathes the spirit of a new Beatitude : BLESSED is the land whose sons are all boys and whose daughters are all girls.

TWO RIVERS AND TWO SHIPS.

I'VE seen such rivers rolling down
  The world I thought them traveling seas,
So vast they made the land look lone,
  And spreading wide their seamless robe
Defied the barrier and the breeze
  To circumnavigate the globe.
I've seen such ships with piles of cloud
  Three heavens deep among the pines
  Stayed with the web of spidery lines,
So queenly fair, so kingly proud,
  It took my breath to see them sail
  So near the sky's blue valance veil
  They might have heard an angel's hail.
And yet they never thrilled and warmed
Until my very soul was stormed,
As when the meadow brook was passed
  With shouts of joy by pilgrims bold
  That played the Israelites of old —
The girls with cambric frocks half-mast,

The boys' blue trousers at the knee,

And twinkling feet walked pebbly street

And so we crossed the mimic sea ; —

As when I launched the dug-out boat

All freighted with the mallow cheese

And saw the jack-knife fabric float

Triumphant in the fresh'ning breeze ;

The little fish like lancets keen

Cut in and out with silver sheen,

The green-legged frog and greener boy

All leap to see the craft go by,

The sweet-flag waves its two-edged blade,

The smoky puff-balls fusillade,

A bob-o'-link rings bells of joy,

A red-bird flashes fire-works nigh,

It is the Fourth of my July,

Until, the cat-tail jungle reached,

My gallant bark careened and beached.

And then we boys and girls sat down

And from a chip hat's battered crown

Shook out, while every tongue was whist,

Some nut-cakes with the good old twist,

I ask like Oliver "for more ! "

Some apples red and water-core,

AND THEN IN BLISS THE BEVY SAT,
AND ALL IN CONCERT STRANGELY MUTE
WITH ROASTING EARS WE PLAYED THE FLUTE.

Some ribb'd and amber gingerbread,
Some roasted corn — ah, what a head
It must have been to fill the hat ! —
And then in bliss the bevy sat,
And all in concert strangely mute
With roasting ears we played the flute.

One boy turned judge and sentenced men
    To die who then were yet unborn,
And one who heard and heeded when
    "Boots and saddles" blew the bugle-horn ;
A sabre kissed him and the scar
Was lighted with a golden star.
One girl for whom the angels sent
Did hear the message, smiled, and went
So long ago nobody knows
Just where she takes her last repose.
Another lives.   Her silver hair
    Is shining with to-morrow's dawn,
Her mournful eyes are full of care.
    Which best? Who knows? Brave heart, live on !

OLD-FASHIONED SPRING.

GIVE me the sweet old-fashioned Spring,
Dear as a girl's engagement ring—
I hear the keys in crystal locks
Slow turn to let the rivers run
And shine like lizards in the sun.
I watch the rigid world come to,
The skies come off with broods of blue,
The soft clouds troop in fleecy flocks,
The mosses green the umber rocks,
The twin leaves lift their tips of ears,
The rushes poise their slender spears,
The squirrels tick like crazy clocks,
The sunshine leave the Southern hall
And swing around to the Northern wall.

I watch the blue smokes slowly rise
Amid the maples' reddening skies—
The hemlock couch, the rafter rails,
The neck-yoked Libras with their pails,

The bended twig, a ghostly spoon,

That films across like a cloudy moon ;

The white eggs dance in the tumbling sap,

The nut-cakes heap a checkered lap,

The young moon's sickle reaps the stars,

Her light ribbed off with maple bars ;

The laugh of girls, the camp-fire glow,

The great black cauldron, bubbling slow,

The amber mouth-piece on the snow —

Oh, memories of the maple fane,

Wax sweet for aye though moons shall wane !

I tread brown earth with loving foot,

   Its breath steals up with Agur's prayer.

I see the lily's green surtout

   Unbutton to the light and air.

I hear the hymn-book songs begin

   To fly abroad from windows wide

With notes of lilac-breath thrown in,

   And rhyme and thyme in mingled tide

I hear the bees' small hum-book's drone

   From garden bed to clover glade

And frogs strike up with deep trombone,

And lilting bells and tambourine

   The old Homeric serenade.

GIVE ME THE SWEET OLD-FASHIONED SPRING.

Give me the dear long-coming
    Spring,
Horizons like a blue-bird's
    wing ;
I love its sights and sounds
    and scents,
    The plowshare's fragrant
    corduroy,
    The greenwood's rustling
    halls of joy,
Down to the toad-stools'
    tiny tents.

I HEAR THE BEES' SMALL HUM-BOOK'S DRONE.

The fire-fly brings his lantern light
To show the summer's velvet night.
The beds of pinks are bright with thrums

THE GREAT BLACK CAULDRON BUBBLING SLOW.

And golden glow chrysanthemums,

Verbenas burn, geraniums blaze,

The smoke-tree clouds with purple mist,

The fuchsia wears an amethyst —

A ruby at the hum-bird's throat

And silver in the finch's note

And satin on the martin's coat,

And fire upon the red-bird's wing,

God speed the June! The Sun is king.

THE ONE STEP MORE.

I.

NOVEMBER'S rude and sleety drummers
Are trampling down the fallen Summer's
Rent uniforms of buff and red,
And crape clouds all the world o'erhead
As if this very world were dead!
The gray drum-majors of the rain
Are beating every window-pane
That shows a ghostly·face again.

II.

Then up the road that shadows blotted
Till all the dark was leopard-spotted,
There shone a dim and twinkling light
As if the sad disastered night
Had shaken down with blow or blight
Amid the gloom and rain and wood
Some star of faintest magnitude.

III.

Poor fire-fly strayed from domes of azure,

Poor taper dropped from God's embrasure,

So tossed and drifted round about

To flutter wild and flicker out

And leave the night in deeper doubt.

Poor lost, forlorn, electric spark

To quench in rain and drown in dark.

IV.

It rounds like daisies broadly blowing
In California's floral snowing.
   The glimmer is a growing gleam,
   The gleam a glow, the glow a beam,
   As dawns afar Cyclopic steam.
   I see its planetary face,
   Its small horizon's curve of grace.

V.

I see a lantern boldly swinging,
I hear its bearer bravely singing.
   His steps as sure upon the sod
   As if the cloudless hosts of God
   Beheld him as he walked abroad.
   No idle speculative eyes
   Are lifted to the clouded skies.

VI.

A little day the boy is bearing
-   For rain and darkness little caring,
   All safe within his home-made noon
   What is Arcturus or the moon
   To him that sings his Bonny Doon?

Within the candle's curving shore
His next step ljes—he needs no more.

VII.

A lantern with a soul to man it
Will light you round the stormy planet.
On that one step all steps await—
March on, my lad! The hour is late—
Another step—*click* goes the gate,
The hearth-blaze shines along the floor,
The light flares out from open door,
The goal is gained with the one step more.

THE BEAUTY OF DEATH.

O II ! Nature loves her children, how the fond
Blue Heaven is hovering all beyond
The bended brim of our full-jewelled day,
Till earth to azure softly melts away.
In her great bosom there is room for all,
For titled lord and trembling leaf to fall ;
Her clouds are anchored and her rains are shed,
O'er lilies faded, as o'er princes dead ;
The mournful murmur in the River's song —
The Bird's lament — to both alike belong.
Dear Mother of us all ! How very small
A place thou need'st for human pride and all
Its jewelry — our treasures, one by one,
Sparkle like rain, and sparkling — they are gone.
They say the Indian Summer is the breath
Of myriad leaves descended to their death.
Ah ! sweet and rare the dying that can shed
The smile of June o'er gray November's dead !
To be a leaf and lie upon the breast

Of summer air — to roof a cup of song,

    That by and by should seek the morning cloud,

And glide from dawn to dawn in melody along,

    And sing at Heaven's portals out aloud ;

To be a leaf, and put a glory on

For dying in — when gentle winds are gone,

To loose the tenure on the forest's crest,

And winnow earthward to a breathing rest —

Would be thrice blest, if this be all of life —

These tardy dawns, these struggles and this strife,

These hopes deferred, these clouds out-biding rain,

The beating bosom and the throbbing brain,

That have no Sabbath, in Time's weary train.

But those spent billows where the loved were laid,

Where smiles were few, and long "good nights" were said,

Where tears were shed, and prayers were made, and song

    Was sung. Oh! never dream the dead are there.

Nature endures, indeed, but not for long,

    The peopled grave. The summer wind shall bear

Its wakened beauty to the air of God.

    Something of loveliness within a shroud

We folded, and we hid it 'neath the sod.

    Nature shall find it, and from clod to cloud

Shall waft it. The summer wind on its sweet wing

Shall bear it round the world. How she shall mould

That dust of ours! The emerald Spring

Shall wear it, and the blue brocade of gold

Wherein blest Autumn blushes like a bride,

Shall have for warp and woof, a ravelled thread

From that old robe of ours we laid aside.

Is this a dying? This a being dead?

The latest fabric from the looms sublime

Hath nothing fairer than that old shall be.

One treasure from thy halls, O gentle Time!

Give us thy graves! 'Tis all we ask of thee!

Through the wide arc, from seraph down to sod,

That dust shall vibrate 'neath the breath of God.

'Tis joy to know these weary hearts we wear,

Shall beat in Nature's greater bosom still;

'Tis bliss to feel there is no "vacant chair"

In earth's dear homestead. "I feel," the poet said,

"The daisies growing o'er me." The dying child

Of song, obedient bent his gentle head,

And died. Oh! no, not died — those flowers that smiled

Around his grave, were springing from his heart;

Dear thoughts of his that could not all depart.

Oh! never seek the dead in billowed graves;

Like sweet stars sprinkled on the rolling waves,

They are but shadows—death in brief disguise,

Look anywhere but there.   May be the skies

Retain them, or the air and light of God.

    The drop of rain that glitters on the leaf —

The dewy world, that satellite of sod,

    Were once perhaps right eloquent of grief;

Nature distilled them, and they would not stain

    An angel's cheek.   If angels ever weep

For joy, well might it be in such sweet rain,

    Where married days lie side by side asleep—

Where night's divorce forever is withdrawn,

And double mornings brink unclouded dawn.

It is not life that stains the window pane ;

    That dimly floats upon the azure air ;

For God did link the labyrinthine chain

    Round something nobler than the garb we wear.

We make the grave the Mecca of the thought —

We dream that beauty there has come to naught ·

As if the rain that glitters gaily down

The bended day wherewith God binds the frown

Of tempests, would linger 'mid the seven,

And hang suspended in an empty Heaven.

The birds that there in green recesses sing,

    Within the maple swinging overhead,

.

May bear away upon each glossy wing,

Some trait of beauty that we fancy dead.

The rose-tree blooms above the sunken grave ;

Her lips are pale below; perhaps they gave

The mantling blush those roses wear to-day —

Their breath the fragrance that they waft away.

We build the tomb — we dream we dyke out day

And fling a gloomy fortress round decay ;

But Nature finds the idle dust we hide —

She cleaves our marble and she mocks our pride.

The hungry air devours the bolts and bars —

The mournful rains slow weep the walls away —

Time's busy fingers part a glimpse for stars,

And darkness yields the tenantry to day.

The grim old pyramids — the mountain caves,

Where one by one the ancient dead were laid,

Like ocean sands behind receding waves

Bear not a trace that human footfall made.

Dead ? What is dead ? Call we disrobing death —

The "little sleep" that thought and heart may take —

The "little sleep" a whisper or a breath,

The morning light or falling rain may break ?

Oh! no. The great High Admiral who guides

Life's fleet, and sets His signal on the tides,

For leaves that drift—who pilots in the day

And leads the ivy on its winding way,

Will bring true Thought, however toss'd and driven,

Clasped round with glory, to the port of Heaven

If there are those who do not dare to die,

 And who would dread to see this great blue tent

Of God slow closing like a dying eye,—

 No hand to fold—no foot-print where they went

Who passed away, then let them rock a thought,

From youth to manhood on the naked breast;

A living thought that shall become the guest

Of Time, and to all heart, and right, and truth,

Take up and breathe for aye the prayer of Ruth.

It is as if the lark ascending nearer God

 Should leave some fragment of his song below—

As if dear June should leave upon the sod

 A flower or two, to part December's snow.

The Summer and the Bird would not be dead ;

One only passed, and one just overhead ;

The Lark would sing while Earth had heart to hear,

And June would linger through the deathless year.

THE CALI-
FORNIA YEAR.

BEYOND the mid-
land Rocky Range
That wrinkles up the
rugged world,
Where gray volcanoes
sat and smoked
Like burgomasters weird
and strange,
And watched the columns as they curled ;—
Where old Decembers crowned and cloaked
Have seen a thousand Junes go by,

A thousand winters leave the line
  Cast down upon the rocks to die,
    Until the granite crags grew white
    With icy bones and Arctic light
And grave-clothes decked with pine ;—
Where grim Sierra shows her teeth,

Medusa East, Minerva West,
A nursing Boreas at her breast,
The chained and halted years beneath,
    She fronts two worlds with pale intent
    And smiles across the Continent.

Beyond her California lies

At graceful length with Zone undone,

Behold this Cleopatra's eyes

Grow azure under Western skies ; —

   Her smitten cheeks turned one by one

   Like rare-ripe peaches to the sun ;

A June of Junes in either hand,

   Her early roses light the late

      To bed, and not a flower to grieve

      From Easter Morn to Christmas Eve —

A tropic heart, a bosom fanned

   By breezes from the Golden Gate.

      Then throned upon the unbound wheat

      She slips her sandals, and her feet

      Walk white among the lilies, while

      We tramp the snow-drift's silent mile.

Her months like Graces stand in groups,

To cull a flower November stoops,

   December's lips with berries stained

      Are pressed upon the cheek of June,

   October's hand is violet-veined

      And morning-glories last till noon.

The Year's four seasons tossed and strown

   Like Sybil's leaves along the track

HOUSE OF REFUGE.

Of Time — the dear old reckoning gone
 For May meets August
  coming back,
And tender blades and yellow sheaves
 In one rich landscape
  strangely met,
 A wild Arabian-night
  vignette,

And winter woods wear flowing sleeves,
 And bud and bloom and harvest all
  Commingle in a carnival.

A VISION OF HANDS.

Y, give all honor to the man
Whose sturdy work sweats off the tan,
Who furrows out the royal road
Where broad-tread harvests march abreast

In rustling robe and golden vest,
And gains his bread first-hand from God ;

Lives hand and glove with out-door life,

Lives hand in hand with faithful wife,

Strikes hands with earnest men who strive

To keep both soil and soul alive ;

Who does his duty out of hand

And tills his heart and feeds his land ;

Is hand to hand against the wrong,

    And sometimes, tallest when he kneels,

    Will lend a hand to roll the wheels

Of manful, mindful toil along.

There is a stain but not of dust

    That soils a hand beyond repair,

The " damnéd spot " of broken trust ;

    There is a fairer hand than fair,

There is a shapelier hand than Burns

    Has sung. It may be broad and brown,

    And knotty as an antlered crown —

The open hand that never turns

    Its back when need is at the door ;

The hand that feels the left-breast knock

    Like flails upon a threshing-floor,

And closes like the Arab rock

    And strikes for undefended Right

    With soul and sinew tense and tight,

Straight out, and smites Goliah down —
I think that hand has won renown ;
Might touch and grace a kingly crown !

The plighted hand that glances white ;
The royal hand with diamond light ;
The gentle hand that cools the brow
Like whispers from the fragrant snow
   Of orchards blossoming in May ;
The artist hand that halts the sun
   To dawn along the canvas gray ;
The hand whose tuneful fingers run
   Along the strings as zephyrs play,
     And float the soul on some sweet dream
   Of peace for which we ever pray ;
   The cunning hands that delegate
     To nerves of fire and pulsing steam,
To lively valve and nimble wheel,
   To things that never want nor wait,
To things that never lie nor steal,
Alive as life and trained and taught
The work by human sinews wrought —
Ah, all these hands are wondrous fair,
And yet recounting all, I dare
   To toast the Farmers' hands that kept

The wolf and wilderness at bay
Where Pilgrims' bristling winters slept,
And shaggy, white-maned lions lay ;
Who picked the flint and picked the flint
For Indian corn and Indian foes,

And cleared the cabins and the rows
Of weeds and wampum by the dint
Of rude flint-locks and rugged hoes.

The hands that fired the morning gun

Of Freedom when the world struck "one,"

And dug their rations as they went

And left the Lord to pitch their tent,

Were Farmers' sons. I rather think

They stood so close to Glory's brink

That, one step more, they would have seen

Headquarters of the sons of men!

Twins of the million hands that donned

　　The hickory shirts and blouses blue,

And marched "with equal step" beyond

　　The solemn dead-lines duty drew;

When soulless reapers took the field

　　And tireless threshers smote the grain,

　　　　And speechless mowers swept the swath

While gallant squadrons charged and wheeled,

　　And bolts of thunder struck the plain,

　　　　And batteries tore a ragged path

　　Through solid columns massed amain

　　　　And mowed the human aftermath,

And Blue and Gray alternate reeled,

And Gray and Blue alternate kneeled

　　Along the road of wreck and wrath.

"WHO GOES THERE?"

The Sun set red as if he wrought

The bloody work he looked upon ;

The Moon rose white as if she caught

The pallid stare on which she shone

Of dead men's faces turned supine

And broken pitchers stained with wine.

"AND FORBID THEM NOT."

IT is May among the blossoms but November in my breast,
There's a warble in the lilacs but my bird has left the nest,
Not a path upon the planet that her little feet have pressed.

Sure an angel must have halted on an errand going by,
Must have whispered to the truant and have taught her how
   to fly,
And she followed up the flutter of his pinions to the sky.

From the Babel of my sorrow she has stolen out the song,
She was tangled in our heart-strings and she took our hearts
   along
With her clinging hands so delicate and yet so wondrous
   strong.

As the reapers miss the daisies when they sweep the golden
   grain
And they rise like constellations when the day begins to wane,
So has Death just missed my darling and she surely lives
   again.

133

Ah, how strange that in her dying she became a deathless
child,

Like the children in the story upon whom the Savior smiled,

That eighteen hundred years and more the ages have beguiled.

She has conquered sin and sorrow, she has triumphed over
time,

Though the sexton told the story when he rung a single
chime,

Yet the echo of her little life shall linger like a rhyme,

And shall turn the thoughts to music that we think in dreary
prose,

And this breath of being rounded till it scarce outlived a
rose,

As the rivulets are woven till the river seaward flows,

With our own be ever blended till the dream of earth shall
close.

PRAIRIE LAND.

THE prairies are the empty beds
  Deserted on some nameless day
By seas that raised their crested heads
  And took their crystal clothes away.
Not empty now! A grander tide
Than those of old that ebbed and died,
  Of golden seas that cannot drown,
Of oceans where no Clarence lies,
All rustling round the loving skies
  That fit the shore-line like a crown.

These feeble images convey
No picture of this realm to-day,
Ye golden seas and tides away!

Behold the stately Northwest stands
  A queenly figure, firm, compact
  In one great grandeur by the act
  Of God and man. One splendid fact,

As if the marble statue woke

Completed at a single stroke —

'Tis thus to me the Northwest stands

    And fronts the hungry world, to hear

The prayer of Christendom for bread,

And holds the answer forth in both her hands!

    The heaping harvests of the year

Upon her prairie palms are spread

    From parallel to parallel.

    The lines that gypsies read to tell

A fortune, are by fortunes hid

As Pharaoh by pyramid.

The men still live who might have seen

    This land without a yesterday —

An empire of unfurrowed green,

Unpeopled paradise of bees,

    Unsown, unmown, unknown, and gay

With floral aborigines;

An empty wilderness of grass

As silent as a looking-glass.

The prairie schooners' canvas white

    Like eggs of ants in beaded line

A COIN OF THE REALM.

Would creep all day, all day in sight,

As blossoms on a creeping vine.

Sometimes the drowning sun would turn

That white to crimson as he loomed,

Would watch to see the canvas burn

Like Moses' Bush all unconsumed;

Would make a trinket of the train,

Then slowly sink beneath the main.

Oh, world so utterly alone!

Oh, nights that weep and winds that moan!

Sometimes a group of horsemen tall

Would ride with day-time at their backs,

Their slender shadows weirdly fall

In strange eclipse along their tracks;

Ride on before like ghosts that guide

And leave no foot-prints as they ride;

Wolves turn and look a glittering growl

And slowly winks the prairie owl,

Till naked Night lets down her hair

And lies along her level lair.

THE DESERTED HOMESTEAD.

IT is clean gone at last—the old homestead! It has forgotten its vernacular. Its household words are no longer the accents of Mother Country but of Faderland. The Dutch have taken it. It is Holland, and the old "turbulent tides" of memory will soon be diked out forever.

But whatever becomes of it, it has helped mankind. "How far that little candle throws its beams; so shines a good deed in this naughty world." Did you ever see a rainbow die?—the sort of architecture that must be repaired every second, or it will crumble into atoms of colorless rain. And so the drops one by one fall into their places, the arch changing each instant and always the same, until the rain comes slow, and the tints grow faint, and the Bow goes out, and the cloud is bare of blazonry as if God had never put a seal to the Covenant. True and beautiful homes are drops of rain, and they are the hope of the world.

He is thrice blest who has some mere earthly thing to tie to; a thing made bright and holy by unselfish affections, simple recollections, small sorrows and large delights. A birth-

place is that thing. It is better to have in the family than
a cow or a carriage, or even a castle after the household
birds are grown and flown. A right-hearted man pays out
the line that ties him to the place of his childhood, but he
never cuts it, for so it is he can hold on to *himself*, and keep
all of his mental belongings together. It is a perpetual clue
to his identity.

Many people seem never to know what they have *done*
with themselves ; they have lost so much, forgotten so much,
despised so much, of feeling, affection, faith, hope and desire,
in an ambition to play flying artillery in life's race, that who
they are is a puzzle even to themselves. This calamity
never happens when you have that place to tie to. The
immortal tramp, Bunyan's Pilgrim, would tell you, if he
could, that a man travels stronger and freer under a knapsack, if only it is not the pack of sin, than when he travels
light. Let everybody, therefore, make a bundle of childhood
and homestead and take them along. They are burdens only
as wings are: only lift *them* and they will lift *you*.

THE DESERTED HOMESTEAD.

FULL twenty summer-times ago
    I walked along this country road,
When life and love were both in blow
    And none would dream it ever snowed.
I saw a schoolma'am coming down,
Her rippling hair was golden brown,
I saw her firm and slender hand,
I saw her foot-prints in the sand,
A pair of rhymes in dainty type
    That brought to mind the old Gazette
Where village poets used to pipe —
    The cricket corner where they set
In little letters chirps of song
Whose lines were only cricket long —
And read them off as children tell
A poem by the nonpareil.

II.

I turned highwayman as I stood

  Beneath these oaks now older grown

And cried as ruder robbers would,

  "Thy life and treasure are my own!"

I halted her with love's surprise

And saw my answer in her eyes;

A bee was busy with a flower,

A bird sang low from maple bower,

The old white school-house swarmed with noise;

  We heeded not the babel rout,

The girls knew better than the boys

  What meant the meeting there without,

And smiling stood and watched me hold

  Her hand in mine and ran and told!

And some were mothers long ago

And some caught out in early snow.

III.

Again I walk the road and meet

  Another schoolma'am coming down

Who was not born when I did greet

  Her sister of the golden crown.

I told this story to the girl

And something like a living pearl

Lit up the eyelid of the child ;

She flashed it off and then she smiled.

There should have been a Bow, I thought,

 That sunshine and that drop of rain —

And then the present was forgot

 And perished days returned again.

This thoughtful, sad September day

Has slowly worn itself away,

The sun and moon are face to face,

He wanes in strength, she gains in grace.

IV.

It is not day, it is not night,

 Where are the feet that came and went?

Here stands the homestead still and white

 And silent as a monument.

Its curtained windows in eclipse,

Its white door fast as marble lips ;

Never before were they denied

The summer flowers and hours outside.

Though tides of fragrance always sweep,

 In warmth and light it has no part,

There in the daytime sound asleep

 And empty as a broken heart.

The willow fountain swings and swerves

And flings its leaf-wrought spray in curves;
Strange, since the loved no longer stay
It has not wept itself away.

V.

Here round the house the brown paths ran
    To lichened gate and stoop and well,
Full forty years since they began
    To warm when busy bare feet fell.
The wilderness redeems its own
With clover leaves and plantain strown,
The old meanders dimmed and grassed,
The surge has washed them out at last.
The dry old grindstone, crank bereft,
    Worn like a pebble in a brook,
And little but the axle left,
    Stands idle in that shady nook.
Ah, lusty times when naked arms
That conquer deserts into farms,
Ground off the sickle's edge of wire
'Mid sparks of wit and sparks of fire,
And scythes, swung down from apple limb
Were set upon its rippling rim.
Gone are the arms that turned the crank
And gone the stroke through grasses rank.

THE WILLOW FOUNTAIN SWINGS AND SWERVES,
AND FLINGS ITS LEAF-WROUGHT SPRAY IN CURVES;
STRANGE, SINCE THE LOVED NO LONGER STAY,
IT HAS NOT WEPT ITSELF AWAY.

VI.

The showers have washed the colored light
Of rainbows down upon the place,
The phloxes flame in red and white,
The pansies in their violet grace;
The jaunty jaybird's azure flash,
The rubies of the mountain ash,
The dear old aster's gay cockade,
The maples with their green parade,
The yellow daisies prim and clean,
The orange butternut that pays
In golden leaves of spotted sheen
Its early dues to Autumn days,—
All these no weary heart can wile
Like loving smiles from living eyes
That light the Lord's last holy mile
To perfect peace and Paradise!

VII.

Ah, flood-wood wreck, old cider-mill!
With apple cheese and amber flow,
Where used to gather round thy rill
The boys and bees of long ago.
How sweet new apples make the air
As fragrance in a maiden's hair.

I see their constellations gleam

Like planets in a fairy's dream,

As if the Maker should baptize

Each new-born star He bade arise

In rare perfume, and all should shine

With aromatic light divine!

VIII.

In silence standing on this brink

Of desolation and decay,

Now in this amber cup I drink

To the dear dead and gone away.

COMO LA SOMBRA
HUYE LA HORA

THE GARDEN THERMOMETER.

LO, a silver pulse in a crystal vein
        And it silently ebbs and flows,
And marks the chill of the North wind's will
        And it times the bloom of the rose.

And it tells of snow in the spotted air,
        And it shrinkingly shows the sift
Of frosty stars where the crimson spars
        Of the Arctic admirals lift.

When the silver mounts in the vein of glass,
        Then the butterfly's wing'd brocade
Shakes out of reef like a folded leaf
        And the corn ranks off in brigade.

When the silent pulse to the Zero sinks
        Then as brave as a lord's saloon
The nail-heads shine in the walls of pine
        Like the dew-drops under the moon ;

And the kitchen fire is an oriflamme
And the panes of the window show
The astral bloom and the diamond plume
And the mimic May of the snow.

There are fans of pearl, there are shells with rings,
There are violets ghostly white,
And tarns and urns and the fretted ferns
Of the winter-time in the night.

There is naught so cold in the Arctic zone
As a heart that is "ten below"
At the snowy line of the dwindling pine,
On the· glacier field or the floe.

And no Boreal blast from its ghastly gloom
Is as chill as the frosty-souled
With thoughts as clear as the Windermere
And the heart left out in the cold.

Let us pray for hearts with an endless June
Though the winds of the world are wild,
No zero there nor a fever'd care
But the blue-eyed faith of a child.

THE MINGLING OF THE NATIONS.

A MEMORY OF THE CENTENNIAL, 1876.

D EAD and gone Truth's faltering lisper
    Rent the recantation robe,
Galileo's feeble whisper
    Rings around the startled globe.
Tremble out the joy, ye steeples,
    While your iron welkins roar,
Met and mingled, Babel peoples
    Sundered by the seas no more.
Met and mingled! Turban, tartan,
    Lotus Egypt, lily France,
Moslem, German, Spaniard, Spartan,
    South Sea Isles from tropic trance,
Lapland snow-drops, Persian roses,
    Grecian laurel, English oak,
Erin's shamrock, land of Moses,   .
    Cedars where the Savior spoke ;
Palm and pine and Judah's willows,
    Grand Brazil whose rainbows broke,

Showering all her leaves with light,

Arctic with his marble billows,

Dead and pallid anthracite.

Scotland's thistle, Scotland's Scott,

Robert Burns and Robert Bruce

Who bid all earth "forget-me-not"

And Time flings out his flag of truce!

Land of Hamlet, hills of Homer,

Almond eyes and Saxon hair,

Alps of Tell and sands of Omar,

Ivory land and Northern Bear.

Gliding on with Orient greeting

See blue-trouser'd thatched Japan

Cool with palm-leaf breezes, meeting

Ermined Russia with a fan!

Palmetto, Ophyr, Oregon,

Call the roll of nations off

From Herr and Don to China John,

From Malabar to Malakoff,

Egypt! Earth's own eldest daughter,

Colorado, silver bride,

One mountain-born and one of water,

Eldest, youngest, side by side.

In and out the halls of wonder,—

Centennial grand the ground,

Mingled nations passing under

    Flags of all the globe around,

Coming, smiling, greeting, going,

Flags above them flaming, glowing,

Like October's frosty woods,

    Gathered like the Judgment Day,

    Like the tides in Fundy's Bay,

Ebb and flow the Multitudes.

And above them, ay, above them,

    Dearer than the Unicorn,

Forty million hearts to love them,

    Fairer than the Crescent Horn,

Like sacred fire on altar-place,

    Lily-white and red as Mars,

Like some broad wing of angel grace

    Brightly flare the Stripes and Stars!

There, in clear or cloudy weather,

    Be it day or be it night,

Ever shine they altogether,

    Stricken sparks of empire light.

"What o'clock by time sidereal?"

    Hark, the world's gray sentries cry.

Behold that banner blue ethereal

    And the Stars shall make reply.

Over all, " Old Glory " gleaming,

Whiter than the driven snow,

Fairer than an angel's dreaming,

Woven in no loom below,

With an Olive Branch upon it

And a Christmas Holly spray,

Words far sweeter than a sonnet

Written with a sunshine ray :

Glory unto God forever !

Hosanna to the Lord again !

Battle blast the nations never,

Peace on earth — good will to MEN.

WELCOME HOME.

THE dust of John Howard Payne, having been borne across the world, was consigned, on a pleasant day in June, 1883, to its final rest in the District of Columbia. The spirit that christened him John Howard, after the great philanthropist, seems prophetic, for it named the boy, that "father of the man," who in the coming time should write out, in simplest household words, the heart of the home-loving world, and so prove himself the gentle lover of the bond and the free. The incident by the Rappahannock river strikingly shows that "Sweet Home," of all earthly melodies, is the master song.

WELCOME HOME.

OH, dews and flowers of splendid June,
    With pearls and garlands grace his tomb
Who taught Milan's dear Maid the tune
That times the whole world's loving feet,
To which all golden hearts shall beat,
    Where'er they wait or weep or roam,
    Of "Home, sweet Home" forever.

O'er mariner on the Spanish main,
    The tattered miner in his tent,
The wanderer on the throbbing plain
Where yellow noons by simoons wheeled
Smite Desolation's flinty shield,
    A second Bow of Hope is bent
    In "Home, sweet Home" forever.

And when to bugle and the blast
    Where battle turns the lilies red,
Through flashing columns standing fast
The soldier cuts the narrow lane
That lets him through to Glory's fane

He hears an angel overhead
Sing "Home, sweet Home" forever.

The weary traveler who waits
In twilight's dim and drear abode
The opening of the Pearly Gates
That some faint ray or friendly star
May shine abroad through doors ajar
And show his fading eyes the road,
Sighs "Home, sweet Home" forever.

A camp of Blue, a camp of Gray,
A peaceful river rolled between,
Were pitched two rifle shots away,
The sun had set the West a-glow,
The evening clouds were crimson snow,
The twinkling camp-fires faintly seen
Across the dark'ning river.

Then floated from the Federal band
The "Spangled Banner's" starry strain,
The Grays struck up their "Dixie Land,"
And "Rally Round" and "Bonny Blue"
And "Red and White" alternate flew,—
Ah, no such flights shall cross again
The Rappahannock river!

And then, above the glancing "beam
Of song" a bugle warbled low

Like some bird startled from a dream
" Home, Home, sweet Home," and voices rang
And Gray and Blue harmonious sang —
    All other songs were like the snow
Among the pines when winds are stilled,
And hearts and voices throbbed and thrilled
    With "Home, sweet Home" forever.
No matter what the Flag unfurled,
Ah, DULCE DOMUM rules the world!

Sweet Singer of the Song of men,
    Thou comest late to claim thine own,
But when the daisies rise again
Arrayed in all thy borrowed dust,
The world will hold thy words in trust
    And Ages chant from zone to zone
    Thy "Home, sweet Home" forever.

The Memnon murmured song, they thought
    When dawning day his lips impressed,
And flushing marble warmed and caught
The sweet Ionic of the Greek ; —
Ah, truer far *thy* lips shall speak
Nor wait the touch of sun or stars,
For thee the night-time has no bars —
    Welcome dear Heart and take thy rest
    At "Home, sweet Home" forever.

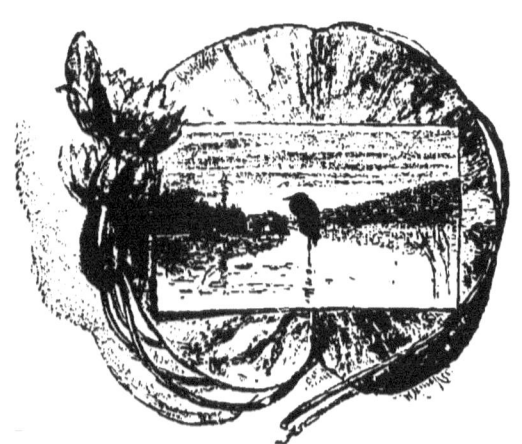